A native of Oklahoma, Patricia Barnes Werner now resides in New York City. She runs a graphic arts business with her husband.

IF TRUTH BE KNOWN

Susan Franks, research director of the Association for Honesty in Government, was involved in one of its biggest cases. Law-enforcement agencies were suspected of circulating false reports on private citizens. Susan was to present her findings to a congressional subcommittee. After meeting Geoffrey Winston, she wasn't sure if they shared a dynamic attraction — or if he would use his position as a congressman to undermine the AHG: he had warned her not to dig too deeply into the matter. Susan did investigate further. When the case proved to have international ramifications, she desperately hoped Geoffrey wasn't involved . . .

Books by Patricia Werner
Published by The House of Ulverscroft:

THE WILL
PRAIRIE FIRE

PATRICIA WERNER

---◆---

IF TRUTH
BE KNOWN

Complete and Unabridged

ULVERSCROFT
Leicester

First published in Canada in 1985

First Large Print Edition
published 2006

All the characters in this book have no existence
outside the imagination of the author and have no
relation whatsoever to anyone bearing the same name
or names. They are not even distantly inspired by any
individual known or unknown to the author, and all
incidents are pure inventions.

British Library CIP Data

Werner, Patricia
    If truth be known.—Large print ed.—
    Ulverscroft large print series: romance
    1. Political corruption—Fiction
    2. Romantic suspense novels
    3. Large type books
    I. Title
    813.5′4 [F]

    ISBN 1–84617–447–3

Published by
F. A. Thorpe (Publishing)
Anstey, Leicestershire

Set by Words & Graphics Ltd.
Anstey, Leicestershire
Printed and bound in Great Britain by
T. J. International Ltd., Padstow, Cornwall

This book is printed on acid-free paper

To Mother and Helene

Prologue

The five men sat at one end of a large polished oak table in the semidarkened room. A ventilation system quietly removed the cigar smoke almost as soon as it was exhaled. The stocky man sitting at the end of the table hunched his shoulders, pulling his gray serge jacket up around his thickset neck. His cheeks were flabby, and the wrinkles in his face betrayed his age, but with his sharp eyes and commanding tone of voice, he retained his authoritative manner — a manner ingrained forty years ago.

He spoke sharply to the other men in his heavy French accent. 'The AHG is getting too close, stirring up trouble among citizens we've had no protest from before. They must not be permitted to disrupt the smooth running of our organization.' He paused to let his words sink in as three of the other four men squirmed in their leather upholstered chairs. These three looked away from him, unsure what they would be asked to do.

Only the thin man with the long, aristocratic nose jutted his narrow chin

1

forward, his smallish eyes still pinned on the Frenchman.

The Frenchman continued. 'There is, in particular, a snoopy young lady who must be discouraged from looking our way.' He looked to his right, retaining the attention of the heavyset, pockmarked man. Then his eyes slid down the table as he addressed the dark-complected fellow with thick black hair.

'Their leader refuses to cooperate now. He shouldn't be too hard to persuade, with what we have on him. But he needs to be watched. You know what to do?'

The dark man nodded, a glint in his black eyes.

The Frenchman looked to his left at the light-haired lad with a red scar under his right eye, the only man in the room who could be called handsome. This man had proved himself in the past. He would do so again.

The thin man with the aristocratic nose leaned forward, ready for instructions.

'You are our link,' said the Frenchman. 'These intruders will appear before Congress soon. You must stop them. Report back to me in detail. I want to know what they're up to, especially the girl.' He paused. 'And if she continues to snoop — well, discourage her. I think you know how.'

The man nodded, flicking an imaginary

speck of dust from the white sheet of paper before him.

'Do not draw attention to yourselves. I don't want our operation exposed. We can't afford any publicity.'

The five men sat quietly. The three younger men were primed for this kind of work. The other two were older, but their experience only added to their craftiness. And they all had confidence in their leader, the Frenchman who considered himself Old World.

Now that the success of their movement was at stake, nothing could go wrong.

1

Susan Franks eyed Ted Branagan as she picked up a persistently ringing phone. Wasn't that just like a man, she thought, as she lifted the receiver. He was leaning back in his swivel chair, feet on the scuffed desk, frowning at a report he was reading. Naturally, he wouldn't think of picking up the phone as long as there was another person in the room to get it.

'Association for Honesty — '

The voice cut her off, preventing her from giving the organization's full name.

'Yes, yes,' said a voice hurriedly. 'I just read your circular. Ten thousand dollars for information leading to the indictment of corrupt government officials. Is that correct?'

Susan looked vaguely in Ted's direction as a smile tugged at her mouth. The amount of the reward had been Ted's idea, and it certainly seemed to be a big draw.

'That is correct,' she said. 'Provided the information you have can be documented and is used in a prosecution.'

'Can it come anonymously?'

She was familiar with this line. 'Not if you

5

want to qualify for the reward.'

A pause. Then, 'Oh, yes. Well, if I come in, I assume confidentiality is guaranteed?'

Susan became all business. 'Yes, of course. The Association for Honesty in Government does everything possible to protect those coming to us with information. The strictest confidentiality is guaranteed.'

Another pause. 'Thank you. I'll call you back.' Then the caller clicked off. Susan looked at the beige receiver in her hand and replaced it in its cradle. Even though the movement for blowing the whistle on government corruption had gained much support, there were still people who were afraid. She shook her head, her dark brunette hair brushing the practical oxford-cloth shirt she wore. People had been intimidated by government bureaucracy for so long that it was hard to break through the wall of fear. 'You can't fight City Hall' had been a maxim forced on people to make them think an individual citizen could do little or nothing about one's grievances.

'Hang up?' Ted's voice broke into Susan's thoughts.

'Yeah.' She shrugged. Then, looking on the positive side, she said, 'Maybe they'll call back.'

'Man or woman?'

'Hard to say. Low voice for a woman, high for a man.'

Ted cocked his head, dropped the papers on the desk and lowered his feet to the floor. 'Still, our batting average is high, considering.'

It took her a minute to realize that he referred to the calls that came in. Since setting up the AHG, whose purpose was to expose waste and corruption in government agencies, they had heard from a variety of people — from civil servants with petty grievances about their jobs, all the way up to former FBI agents who had led them to some major cases that had successfully been brought before congressional subcommittees.

Ted Branagan was the president of the Association for Honesty in Government. An Irish Catholic who had gone to school at the University of Colorado, he had then bummed around Europe for several years before returning to the States. It was then he became interested in the grassroots organization being formed as a watchdog on government corruption. The AHG felt the Justice Department wasn't doing its job, and the group was disappointed that so little had been done to clean up government crimes. There had been a lot of talk after Watergate, over a decade ago now, but little had been done. So the AHG decided to take a hand in the matter. Ted quickly became their leader. By the time Susan had joined six months ago, Ted had been elected chairman; she filled his previous spot as director of research.

Just then the door opened and Cindy Conrad entered, her arms full of paper bags and a carton with iced drinks. Susan rose to help her, and the two women lowered the food to Cindy's desk next to the door. When Ted sniffed the food, he also rose and came toward them.

'I was wondering if we were going to have to serve you,' Susan quipped.

'What?' Ted asked distractedly, opening a bag to search for the ham-on-rye. He obviously hadn't understood her joke. That didn't matter, Susan thought idly. Ted wasn't a male chauvinist; he was just usually so involved in work or thinking about it that receptionist duties fell to Cindy, and Susan picked up the phone or ordered food when Cindy was out.

There were other staff members in their fourth-floor offices. Michael Gunderson and Tammy McShane handled most of the confidential interviews. Susan and Ted followed up on details and prepared their research for the congressional hearings resulting from the evidence brought to them by victims of corruption within various government agencies.

'Pickle?' asked Cindy, who never ate hers. Her round blue eyes and dimpled expression revealed she was oblivious to any undercurrents in the room.

'Oh, thanks,' said Susan. Thinking of congressional hearings, she returned with her tuna-salad sandwich to her desk, which sat at right angles to Ted's, and spoke to him over her shoulder. 'You ready to work on the false-reports issue?'

'Umm,' said Ted as he attempted to swallow a large bite of sandwich. 'I was just going over the Hornstein statement.' He carried his lunch back to his gray metal desk, sat down and faced Susan. 'Want to work out our strategy tonight?'

Susan considered as she chewed her food. It was usually a good idea to wait until after hours so they could work away from ringing phones and questions that had to be handled during the day. This case might prove to be a big one, and it demanded a lot of attention. 'Okay,' she said after she swallowed. 'You want to come over? About seven?'

'How 'bout we do it at my place? We met at your place last time.'

'Doesn't make any difference to me.'

'We can order in,' he said, taking her

indifference to be agreement. His green eyes brightened at the idea, and his wavy black hair fell across his forehead, adding to the charm he naturally exuded when he spoke of something he cared about.

'I like the new Chinese place we ordered from last time,' she commented.

'Done,' he said as the phone rang. Cindy answered, then said, 'It's for you, Ted.'

A trace of a frown dampened his buoyant look as he took the call. Susan returned to her sandwich while she studied a list of names peeking out from under a clip-board on her desk. Recognizing the names as members of the congressional subcommittee that would be hearing the AHG's testimony on false reports, she read the names.

She was familiar with the first three. Part of her job as research director for the AHG was to get the backgrounds on all the subcommittee members: politics, favorite causes, likes and dislikes. The fourth name was new. She would have to do some work there. Then her eyes lit on the fifth name on the list — Geoffrey Winston, Democrat from New Mexico. Her pulse quickened, and she could feel a flush creep up her neck. Yes, she had certainly met Geoffrey Winston, and the pictures tumbled in her mind as she recalled their meeting at a press conference the AHG had given in December.

She and Ted had been fielding questions posed by a substantial group of reporters who had come to a hotel suite at the Watergate Hotel. She had been nervous, but Ted had done this kind of thing before. He would handle most of the questions, only calling on Susan for a few comments. He had said that having a man-woman team representing the AHG would look good. Susan recalled Ted's unabashed appraisal of her looks when she had met him that morning. The large gray silk bow on the front of her lavender blouse, against the deep navy of a perfectly fitted suit, had complemented the dark hair that hung in soft waves about her face. Her subdued eye shadow had emphasized her brown eyes. Ted had looked quite dapper himself in a dark three-piece gabardine suit with dark blue silk tie.

A man leaning against the back wall had caught Susan's attention as he slipped into the room halfway through the press conference. She couldn't see a clip-on badge, and when he asked no questions, she began to wonder who he was. He was tall, broad shouldered, with broad, flat cheekbones. His nose looked a little crooked, as if it had been broken once, but it did not detract from the deep-set penetrating brown eyes. His brown hair was sprinkled with gray. Susan remembered now that she must have found him instantly attractive, though not handsome in the traditional sense.

At the time, she had been too busy to form these thoughts into words. Rather, it had been an instant reaction. She remembered with embarrassment that she had been staring at his brown herringbone suit when he suddenly shot up a hand and Ted called on 'the gentleman in the back.'

'How is the AHG funded?' the strong voice boomed, startling Susan. She could tell he was used to projecting his voice across a room.

'By its members, patrons and sponsors,' Ted said into the microphone. 'In the two years since its founding, the AHG has grown to twenty affiliated chapters throughout the United States. As a nonprofit organization, we rely heavily on contributions. We have an active fund-raising campaign managed by the chapter in New York.'

The man at the back scowled, but he said nothing, and Ted moved on. A little later, one of the reporters in the back row left his seat to whisper with the man who had caught Susan's attention. She was about to turn her attention away from him when she caught him shrugging and gesturing to the reporter that he had no comment. A few more heads turned, and she caught a low mutter from Ted, who had lowered his head away from the microphone. When she looked back, the man was gone.

'Who does he think he is?' Ted grumbled after the press conference as the reporters filed out and Susan and Ted gathered up their materials to leave.

'Who was he?' asked Susan. She remembered her initial reaction to him and was almost embarrassed by her curiosity.

'I didn't recognize him when he spoke,' Ted said to her, shrugging into his tan overcoat, 'but I'm pretty sure that was Congressman Winston from New Mexico. He was on a subcommittee that heard an earlier case of ours.'

She wrinkled a brow. 'But why was he here?'

Ted shook his head. 'Beats me. Curiosity? Wanting to get a fix on us? All I know is that he's been appointed to hear our evidence on false reports.'

'But we didn't even mention that today.' This press conference had been staged because of the AHG's success in recent cases. They wanted to use the press to help them in their fund raising.

Ted shrugged. 'Oh, I can understand it.

Maybe he wanted to find out who we are, what we're like. After all, congressmen have to do their own homework, too.' He didn't say that usually they had their staff do it for them, which was more likely.

Susan didn't know how seriously to take Ted. It was at times like this that he confused her. He seemed to enjoy hearing the way he expressed things, but his words often contained double meanings, and she could not always see behind his words to know what he really meant.

They went downstairs and out to the sidewalk, where taxis were pulling up. A snowstorm had started while they were inside, and Ted went to get his car out of the parking garage. Even though she was standing under the awning of the hotel, snow blew onto her. She turned to look toward the lobby when Congressman Winston stepped out onto the sidewalk right in front of her.

For an instant they stared at each other. She was acutely aware of the fact that his height was perfectly suited to her five feet six inches. She felt snowflakes land on her cheeks and nose and tried to think of something to say. The congressman appeared disgruntled, but as he looked at her, his dark eyebrows arched, and surprise filled his brown eyes. She knew she was staring at him, but it would be rude simply to turn away, so she nodded, swallowing the dry, cold winter air as she did so.

He cleared his throat, brushed some of the snowflakes from his face and took a step toward her. 'You're Miss — '

'Franks,' she managed to say. Then, after a pause, during which he scrutinized her, she said, 'You were at the press conference.'

He seemed annoyed again as he answered, 'Yes. Oh, forgive me. I'm Geoffrey Winston.'

'Nice to meet you, congressman,' she said, extending a gloved hand for him to shake. He took the hand in his own firm grip, and the leather of his glove crushed against hers as they formally shook hands. She didn't know what to say next. She wanted to ask him what he had been doing at the press conference, but at the same time, she wanted to stare into his eyes. Something about those slightly uneven features fascinated her.

Then Congressman Winston took a few steps forward, glanced out at the snowy street and back at her. About an inch of snow had already accumulated. He looked down at Susan, who had instinctively moved closer to him to get out of the blowing snow, his height and breadth forming a sort of protective shield. For a brief instant their gazes locked at a comfortable angle, and his eyes seemed to soften. His voice, when it came, was deep but less harsh than it had been upstairs. 'Do you have transportation? I'd be glad to drop you off somewhere.'

Susan felt her heart begin to throb in that old familiar way whenever she met a man she liked — someone who held a promise of excitement. For a moment she forgot the circumstances under which she had first seen him and allowed a smile to creep into her large brown eyes and the curve of her lips. 'Thank you,' she said with an uneven flutter in her heart. How long had it been since she'd felt that sensation? 'But I've got a ride.' *I'll take a rain check*, she wanted to say, and then she swallowed her words. She glanced away, curbing the adrenaline that had begun to pump through her. This was too awkward. He was an interesting man, but one she would have to deal with on a business footing. Thoughts of a social encounter were out of the question under the circumstances.

'Susan.'

She snapped her head up, staring at Ted's flashing green eyes. He was hunched over his desk, the phone slung over his shoulder.

'Sorry,' she said, feeling the red flood her cheeks. 'I was thinking.'

'Well, think about an answer to my

16

question instead, will you?' He was obviously baiting her.

'Question?' She grew more embarrassed, appalled at how far her thoughts had strayed. She hadn't been listening at all.

'Yes.' Irritation had taken root in his voice. He stared at her for a moment, punishing her with his look; then he sighed, as if she were a child he had to patronize.

Susan stumbled over an apology. 'What did you ask me? I'm listening now.'

'I said, the appeal has been refused on Clayton Brown's FOIA request to Globenet. Shall we go for judicial review?'

The Globenet request. 'Why, of course. We should move right along to judicial review.'

Ted hoisted the telephone back up to his mouth and spoke into it. 'Hello,' he said. 'Yes, I suggest we take the matter to court.' He waited while the party on the other end responded.

'Yes,' he said again. 'One of our attorneys can request a judicial review for you.'

He waited again, then shrugged, as if the person speaking on the other end of the telephone would see him. 'Of course, should Globenet have a change of heart . . . ' He let the statement dangle.

Then, after a few 'mm-hms,' he hung up. Susan looked at him, her thoughts now gathered back where they belonged.

'So?'

'So,' Ted said, drumming a pencil eraser on his desk. 'Mr. Brown wants our attorney to request a judicial review, since he can't afford a lawyer of his own. I expect Globenet will have a change of heart.' Then he and Susan smiled conspiratorially.

One of the AHG's major accomplishments was learning to use, and then advising others on how to use, the Freedom of Information Act. It was a simple tool, one that ensured the rights of private citizens to obtain access to government agency records that he or she specifically wanted to see — whether or not the agency wanted these records made publicly available. The act itself, passed into law in 1966, looked complex, but it was easy to use. All it took to put it into action was a one-page letter and a postage stamp, plus patience and learning what some of the typical agency responses to a request for information might be. Most important, a citizen did not have to explain his reasons for requesting the files. If a government agency wished to refuse the request, the burden of proof rested with the agency to show why it would not release the information.

Susan and Ted were amused that this particular request had moved to judicial review, because that meant that they were very soon likely to have all, or most of, the documents they had advised their clients to request. Up to now, in all the cases the AHG initiated, the agency that was trying to prevent documents from being released had experienced a change of heart before the matter went to a court hearing. The reason was that a court decision could produce a precedent in favor of the citizen requesting the documents. All contended cases thereafter would most likely be settled in favor of the citizen using the FOIA. But with no court precedent, each citizen requesting files would have to fight the battle all over again.

★ ★ ★

Susan pulled into the garage at the back of the red brick town house where she had rented an apartment in Georgetown for the past four years. She had found the place a year after she'd started working on her library-science degree in night school. By day she had worked in the copyright office of the Library of Congress, saving up enough money to get an apartment of her own instead of having to share with roommates, as she did when she had first come to Washington.

Many of the houses in Georgetown, although at least a century old and built close together, had carriage houses or garages that opened on to narrow alleys. Susan was lucky that parking space went along with her apartment, for street parking in this part of town was impossible to find.

She had stopped at home to drop off some dry cleaning and to freshen up before driving to Ted's place. As she left the garage and walked around the town house, she thought about Geoffrey Winston. She had brought home some clippings she had found about him and wanted to read them over before she had to go to Ted's.

She barely noticed the passersby on P Street, mostly tourists and people associated with nearby Georgetown University. However, her attention was caught by a light-haired man polishing a maroon Toyota Cressida in front of the house next door, and she registered the fact that she'd never seen him in the neighborhood before. It probably didn't mean anything, she told herself. As she opened the door to the town house, the man glanced up. She paused inside the door, looking at him. He was young and handsome despite the disfiguration under his right eye. Then he returned to polishing his car. He was probably a student, or the son of some neighbor, she thought. In a few moments she was in the front door and went up the carpeted stairs that led to her second-floor apartment.

She dropped her purse and the clothes over the end of her motley overstuffed sofa, then slipped out of her coat and unzipped her waterproof boots. She then turned on the gooseneck lamp that curved over the sofa. She returned to the door to retrieve her briefcase and moved toward her large worktable, in the dining area, stacked with notebooks and files. After setting the case on the table, she flicked open the catch and took out the file of clippings.

Time for a cup of tea, she thought, leaving the file on the table and padding in her stocking feet to the tiny kitchen. The branches from the tree at the front of the house scraped on the window overlooking P Street. Like the other streets in this neighborhood near Georgetown University, the brick-paved street was lined with other brick town houses in hues of blue, gray, yellow and brown, with shutters painted in contrasting bright colors. Susan filled the kettle with water and turned on the gas stove. She returned to the dining-room work area and sat down. By now the dampness from outside was beginning to leave her. It was late

March and still blustery.

She flipped open the folder and gazed at Geoffrey Winston staring out at her from the news clipping. His brows were lowered, and a shoulder hitched up as if his arm had been raised to make a point when the picture had been snapped. Even in the black-and-white news photo, the intensity of his gaze seemed to leap off the page, and Susan felt the muscles around her throat tighten.

She had summarized his activities both at the state level and as a U.S. representative to Congress. He was humanitarian but practical, she thought.

The teakettle sputtered and whistled, summoning Susan from her chair. She pushed Geoffrey Winston to the back of her mind and concentrated on the issues she and Ted wanted to discuss later that evening. A number of people had come to the AHG complaining that reports, full of misinformation, were being circulated among various law enforcement agencies, causing harassment to private citizens. The AHG planned to present evidence of false reports to a congressional subcommittee. Susan paused a moment to ponder the issue. Why would anyone bother to clutter the files of U.S. law enforcement agencies with false reports? That was the answer they sought.

When she entered the living room again, the phone was ringing. It was Ted. 'Change in plans,' he said. 'The plumber's still here. There was a leak, and the super let him in. I think it would be better if we met at your place. All right with you?'

'Sure. You can just bring the food with you.' She looked at her watch. 'Have you ordered yet?'

'I'll call now. Pick it up on the way.'

'Oh, Ted, don't leave anything lying around.'

He laughed, understanding her warning. 'Don't worry.' He hung up.

Susan and the rest of the staff had learned to be careful of possible snoops. As far as they knew, no one had ever tried to spy on their plans or harass them in any way. It was somehow a little surprising that no one had. But they had to be careful. Surely there were those in the government who would have their own reasons for not wanting the AHG's whistle-blowing activities to come too close.

★　★　★

Ted hung up the phone and looked around his crowded apartment, scratching the back of his neck as he thought about the materials he'd had in here lately. Nothing confidential, he was sure of it.

He wasn't really a messy person, but the cluttered look helped disguise the fact that he was very careful in his work. The apparent disarray made him look careless, so that anyone checking up on him thought Ted an easy mark. Any spies would drop their guard, thereby revealing themselves. It was an old trick.

He walked toward the bathroom, where a swarthy plumber with thick black hair was changing a valve on one of the pipes.

'Fix the leak?' asked Ted, watching the man work.

'You bet.' The plumber nodded, throwing a new-looking wrench into the toolbox. Ted's eyes raked over him, taking in the sharp crease in his pants and the freshly washed look of his gray work shirt.

'Long day?' asked Ted, leaning against the door frame, waiting for the plumber to finish.

'Oh, yeah,' responded the man, wiping his hands on a clean rag. 'Everybody's got a leak.'

Ted shook his head, making conversation. 'My downstairs neighbors are complaining all the time. They want to know what the odor is that drifts down the air shaft. They complain if I set my alarm too loud. Then this leak — it goes through my floor into their ceiling.' He shrugged. 'What can you do?'

The plumber nodded sympathetically and made ready to leave. Ted stuck out his hand. The plumber took it warily.

'Well, thanks,' Ted said, giving the man a disarming grin. 'See you next time.'

'You bet.'

Ted walked to his window and waited until the plumber left the building and got into the truck parked across the street. New tools, clean shirt. Worked all day?

'He's no plumber,' Ted muttered under his breath.

★　★　★

Thursday morning Susan got off the elevator and walked briskly down the hall to the AHG office. She started to lean over to put her briefcase down so as to retrieve her keys from her handbag but stopped abruptly. The door stood ajar.

Someone must be here already, she thought. She was used to being the first one in, but she wasn't always. She pushed the door in and then gasped.

Ted stood in the middle of the room, his face tight with anger, surveying the wreckage around him. Tables were overturned, and her desk lamp was on the floor, the bulb shattered. The filing cabinets' drawers had been pulled out and thrown on the floor. Everything had been rifled.

'My God,' she exclaimed. 'What happened?'

Ted turned to her and said sharply, 'What does it look like?'

'Who . . . what?' She was too stunned to think.

Just then, the sound of footsteps behind her made her turn around. Tammy came in, stopped, stared and swore. Her face registered the same shock Susan felt.

'Better start going through stuff,' Ted said, kicking aside a wastebasket near his foot. 'Find out what they were looking for. Itemize what's missing. We'll have to report it.'

Susan nodded. From the way the papers were strewn about, it did look as if someone had been searching for something. She picked up her desk lamp and straightened up the things on her desk. By the time Michael and Cindy came in half an hour later, some of the files were back in place.

'Lock's busted,' Ted said, running his fingers over a damaged filing cabinet lock. Luckily, they didn't keep vital documents in these cabinets. They were in the safe in the back. He went to check it.

Susan looked over the list she had

compiled. There were things missing, all right. A typewriter, two calculators, the petty-cash box, some rolls of stamps. She couldn't figure it out. If this was merely a theft, why the disruption of filing cabinets? It took a stretch of the imagination to think the thieves were looking in those cabinets for more office equipment or money to steal.

But none of the files seemed to be missing. Had whoever broken in been after something specific and not found it?

Of course, the safe in the back. As Ted returned from the bathroom, she gave him a look. He shook his head almost imperceptibly. They hadn't found it. She sighed, looking down at her list. Important papers were kept in the safe Ted had had installed behind the medicine cabinet in the bathroom. Susan had been astonished when he'd shown it to her. He had taken some trouble to disguise it. The toiletries had to be removed from the second shelf and a panel slid back to get to the combination lock.

In fact, the whole procedure was so much trouble, she seldom used the safe. But Ted did. The only other person who knew about it was Tammy. There was no real reason to keep Michael from knowing about it, too, but they'd decided the fewer people involved, the better. And Cindy didn't do any confidential work, so she didn't need to know. Neither did the volunteers who helped them out occasionally.

She could tell from Ted's look that the safe hadn't been touched. The police had arrived and were now taking down information on what had been stolen.

'So only these items, nothing else?' asked one of the policemen.

'That's right,' Ted said.

'Seems like maybe they were looking for something else, though, what with these locks busted. You sure there are no papers, documents — anything like that — missing?'

'We don't think so,' said Ted. 'If we discover anything else missing, we'll let you know.'

The cop flipped his notebook shut and nodded to his partner. They were finished.

When they were gone, Ted came over and leaned his hands on Susan's desk. She looked up at him, worried. 'Now what?' she said.

He stood up and shoved his hands in the pockets of his denims. 'Now nothing. We continue doing what we're doing.'

2

Susan rewound the microfilm on its spool and then replaced it in its box. She rotated her shoulders to relieve some of the tension, then pulled her briefcase onto her blue-jeaned lap and slipped a sheaf of papers into it. She had been searching through reels of microfilm for several hours in the library, and had come up with some new information that might be useful in their present case. Even though it was Saturday, she had decided to devote the afternoon to work.

She had been so absorbed that she scarcely noticed the hour, but now aching muscles and eyestrain told her it was time to quit. She squeezed her eyes shut, then looked up at the ceiling to change focus. After doing close work for a length of time, it helped to focus on objects at a greater distance to exercise her eye muscles.

She looked at the farthest corner of the room and then at the desk where she had been about to turn in her microfilm. There, with his broad back toward her, she was almost sure, was Congressman Geoffrey Winston. Susan froze. The wavy brown hair flecked with gray and the straight shoulders seemed familiar, but since she hadn't seen him in nearly four months, she thought briefly that she might be mistaken. Her gaze dropped to the tapered waist and then to the casual brown corduroys he wore that just delineated the lines of firm hips and thighs. He had a light tan corduroy jacket slung over one arm, and he was leaning over the counter, discussing something with the dark-haired woman on duty there.

Susan realized she was holding her breath. She sat straight in her chair again and slowly let the air out of her lungs as she fiddled with her pencil and briefcase, trying not to feel so self-conscious. After a few seconds, she glanced back between the microfilm machines, and her heart skipped a beat. He had shifted his weight to the other leg and had turned his profile to Susan. It *was* Geoffrey Winston. She could see his slightly irregular nose and the eyes and brows that seemed so commanding. She lowered her gaze. It was silly to feel so awkward. Why shouldn't he be in the National Archives? He was probably doing research, too. She had no reason to feel embarrassed at meeting him here.

Slowly she slid back her chair and stood up. She paused, but he didn't leave the desk.

The woman had disappeared, and he seemed to be waiting for her to return, probably with a reel of microfilm. Susan bent over to lift her briefcase, then straightened her back resolutely. With her pulse quickening, she walked around the machines and into his line of sight.

He caught the movement to his left and turned full front. For a moment his eyes were blank, as if he were still concentrating on his own work. But recognition replaced concentration, and then a look of eagerness swept over his face as he leaned forward slightly.

Susan cocked her head and prepared what she hoped was a sociable smile. His eyes lit up as he looked at her, and she felt her blood pressure leap up another notch. Nevertheless, she tried to maintain a business-like exterior as her hand came forward to meet his grasp.

'Miss Franks,' he said, and it seemed he was caught off guard as well. 'I see you're working on the weekend, too.'

She gave a little laugh. 'I didn't have anything else to do.' Then she held her tongue. Why had she put it that way? She shrugged, looking at him, hoping he wouldn't mock her for lacking anything better to do than work on a Saturday afternoon.

He held up a hand in a gesture that said, *You don't have to explain.* Out loud, he said,

'I understand. I admire dedicated workers.' Then he frowned, looking awkward, and Susan suppressed a grin. It was becoming clear to her that they both felt ill at ease with their conversation.

'Say,' he said, 'if you've finished, I'd like to have a few words with you. If you're not busy, that is. My work can wait. Do you have half an hour?' He had regained his poise and had become the smooth politician.

She began to relax a little. 'I have — ' She bit her lip, preventing herself from saying, 'I have all evening.' This time she couldn't quite mask her faux pas and simply stared at him with a look of confusion.

A slow smile spread over his craggy features as he turned from the desk and waved to the woman, who had just looked up from her filing cabinet full of microfilm boxes. He took Susan's elbow. 'Then let's wet our whistles,' he said. 'Could I buy you something to drink — or eat?' he said, as if he realized he was getting hungry and liquid would not be enough to satisfy him.

She smiled straight ahead, enjoying the feel of his hand on her arm as he guided her to the door. She matched her step to his, allowing their shoulders to brush, her broadcloth shirt moving softly against his cotton one as they left the room. At the elevator in the corridor, he helped her into her Windbreaker, then shrugged into his corduroy jacket, for the April weather was still blustery and unpredictable.

As they emerged from the large granite building that housed the National Archives, he steered her in the direction of Seventh Street. 'My car is over here,' he said. 'Did you drive over?'

'Uh-huh,' she said, forgetting where she had parked. Then, remembering, she pointed up the block. Reading the perplexity in her face, he said, 'We could go in my car, and then I'll drive you back to pick up yours.' He seemed to be considering where to take her.

'I live in Georgetown,' she said, feeling embarrassed again. 'If you follow me home, I could park my car, and we could have something nearby.'

He looked relieved. Georgetown offered many possibilities for a casual drink or meal. 'Great. You lead the way.'

Susan gave him a few directions just in case he got lost. Then she walked away from him toward her powder-blue VW Rabbit, not yet allowing herself to contemplate the consequences of agreeing to join Geoffrey Winston for a drink. She only knew she enjoyed the stimulation she felt in his presence. She got into the car, pulled out of her parking space, and waited for his bright red Audi 5000S to round the corner. She wondered if the little sports car was a clue to another aspect of his sober political personality. Then, giving a wave, she pulled out into traffic.

Soon they were moving along Constitution Avenue past the mall. They left the Washington Monument behind and turned onto Virginia Avenue. Susan watched in the rearview mirror to make sure he followed. The Audi stayed steadily behind her. She took a few deep breaths, now contemplating what she had done, wondering if she was courting danger.

She didn't even know why he had asked to talk to her. She frowned as she realized she had said yes before she even knew his intentions. She tried to justify her acceptance of his invitation and waffled between thinking he wanted to talk about business and the fact that he just might find her as attractive as she did him. Then she chided herself. It would be foolish to socialize with Geoffrey Winston on either count. If it was the AHG he wanted to talk about, she would have to be careful. Suppose he wanted to sniff out their plans for the congressional hearing for his own purposes?

They passed the Watergate Hotel on their left, where they had first met, and she felt a ripple of excitement run through her. She took a deep breath to calm the excitement. The AHG had nothing to hide and she'd be safe as long as she didn't say anything that couldn't be backed up with facts and as long as she appeared levelheaded. Perhaps he wanted to test the waters and make sure the AHG knew what they were doing. But there was something wrong with that, she thought. As she swung into the congested traffic on Wisconsin Avenue, she caught the inside of her lip between her teeth and glanced up to see the red Audi take the corner. This was no way to operate. He would hear their testimony at the subcommittee hearing. What good would snooping around ahead of time do?

She raised a brow as she turned into P Street, where it was quieter, and bumped along the brick road. Geoffrey did not follow. Instead, he would park in a lot on Wisconsin as they had arranged. They would meet on the corner. Susan turned on Thirty-fifth Street and then maneuvered into her alley and garage.

She left the car and closed the garage, then walked briskly along O Street. In a few blocks, she spied Geoffrey Winston standing idly near the corner as people passed in and out of an antique shop. Her mind was in turmoil as she approached him, the heels of her boots rapping on the sidewalk at her quick pace. She shook her hair back over her shoulders. It was a natural female desire, she supposed, to want to be found attractive by a virile male. She smiled as she imagined some richly plumed exotic birds prancing before each other. She had to admit that men and women played the mating game just as did the birds and the beasts. Oh, well, she thought wryly, it would be a boring world if we were all the same sex.

Then she reined in her runaway thoughts. She might enjoy his admiring glance, but Congressman Winston was no man to flirt with, she reminded herself. It would be foolish to encourage him, especially in light of their professional association.

He looked so at ease, Susan thought as she approached him. He fit into the surroundings so well. With his relaxed pose and casual clothes, he could pass for a professor in this neighborhood that catered to Georgetown University.

As he saw her, he turned to join her, and they walked on toward the corner. Susan was familiar with many of the eating places along Wisconsin Avenue and Prospect Street. Should she suggest a place, or would he decide?

'Why don't we walk along Prospect?' he said, as if he had divined her thoughts. 'We can pick a place we like, unless you have a favorite.'

'Fine with me.' She glanced at him and saw that he was taking in the sights. It was a colorful street, with its shops, galleries and restaurants. Artists, students, tourists and business people thronged here for entertainment, shopping and just to enjoy seeing the quaint historic buildings and watching the people pass by.

Susan walked comfortably beside Geoffrey on the narrow sidewalk. He held her elbow easily, steering her through the crowd, and it felt, Susan realized with a start, as though they were accustomed to walking together.

This is ridiculous, she told herself. She hardly knew Geoffrey Winston, yet she knew instinctively that she liked him. That was unusual, she thought, for she did not often form an opinion of a person so quickly. She preferred to get to know someone slowly, file her first impression in the back of her mind, and continue to gather data about the man or woman and evaluate the information to see if her later observations matched her first impressions.

She smiled to herself as they paused beside a restaurant and looked inside. In the dark interior she saw red checked tablecloths on round tables.

'I don't know about you,' he said, peering in, 'but I've got an appetite. After a drink, I wouldn't mind a good meal.' Then he turned to her. 'Of course, I may be treading on your time. Did you have plans?'

She thought briefly of Ted, whom she had promised to call after her day of research, but she decided tomorrow would do. Often she and Ted drifted together for Saturday evenings, a carryover from sharing their interests at work, but there was no other reason for them to see each other. She hesitated, though, suddenly afraid to leave herself too open. She squelched her indecision, however, giving way to a desire to share the evening with the congressman. With a quickening heartbeat, she realized she wanted to know more about him. For a moment she felt as if she were teetering dangerously on the brink of an important decision. Then he pulled her out of the way of some pedestrians, and she could smell his woody, pine-scented cologne.

'I had no plans,' she said. 'Dinner would be fine.'

'Good.' She detected a slight easing of tension in him, as if he, too, had felt embarrassed to ask her to accompany him to dinner on a Saturday night on such short notice, when they had only just met. Then another thought tumbled into her mind. What if he were married?

If so, did he have a family here or in his home state? As she contemplated the idea, a feeling of frustration overcame her. She had not expected their relationship to develop in one evening to such an extent that their marital status would become relevant. But as they entered the dimly lit French café, she had to acknowledge inwardly that she had, perhaps, hoped for just that.

Inside the restaurant, pastoral landscapes and modern prints adorned exposed brick walls. They followed the maître d' to an upper level, and they were seated in comfortable cane chairs. Geoffrey seemed pleased with their table, which was positioned near the back of the restaurant, next to the dark red brick wall. The waiter came and lighted the tall white candle in the center of the table.

'Would you like a drink?' Geoffrey asked.

'Just a glass of white wine.' It wouldn't do to lose her head, and a stronger drink might relax her too much. In spite of the response she felt to the man sitting opposite her, she had to maintain her professional decorum.

They both chose a Chablis. Geoffrey rested his arms on the table and leaned toward her, creating an atmosphere of casual intimacy. She smiled, looking into his warm brown eyes. For a moment it was enough for them to face each other comfortably; there was no need to speak.

Finally, Susan shifted in her seat and said, 'You mentioned you wanted to have a few words with me. What did you want to talk about?'

He cleared his throat. 'Oh, I was interested in your work. I hoped you could tell me about the AHG. How did you come to work for them?'

She leaned back in her chair. 'I came to Washington five years ago and got a job at the Library of Congress.' She sighed, running through images of the past in her mind. 'I was always interested in causes, I guess. Civil rights, women's rights. Then I heard of this grassroots project to clean up sectors of the government where corruption and waste had gotten out of control. I went to an open meeting and I met Ted Branagan.'

At the mention of Ted's name, Geoffrey's eyes narrowed slightly, but Susan went on, leaning forward again as her enthusiasm built.

'Our intention is to see that the laws of the government are applied equitably. We want to bring about political reform and to defend private citizens from corrupt and dishonest officials.'

His frown deepened. 'A bit idealistic, don't you think? Taking on the whole government like that.'

Susan shook her head. 'Someone has to do it. Most of the people who work in government are good, honest people. I firmly believe that. But many of them have to condone unethical acts just because they fear harassment otherwise. We provide help for people who want to do something about a situation they know is wrong when they want to step forward and be heard. They know that, as single individuals, they won't be heard, but with the support of the AHG, they can see results if they've really got a case. We're putting the government back where it belongs — in the hands of the people.'

Geoffrey cleared his throat. 'No doubt your intentions are good. There probably isn't a man alive who wouldn't laud your efforts except for the, let's say, two-and-a-half percent minority who, for their own twisted reasons, think that power and controlling others will solve some sort of problem for them.'

She nodded, continuing his analogy. 'The other ninety-seven-and-a-half percent of the population are basically good, only they

41

sometimes get caught up in forces beyond their control.'

Geoffrey leaned forward, lowering his voice. 'But that two-and-a-half percent can be dangerous, Susan.' For a moment, she thought he was threatening her, and she felt startled.

'What do you mean, dangerous?'

'Some cases will never be prosecuted, Susan, even if you gather all the evidence. There are people in very high places who will prevent it.'

'That's exactly what I mean,' she said, angry now. 'The AHG has stepped in because the Justice Department hasn't been doing its job.'

Their flashing gazes locked for a moment, and neither relented until Susan finally shifted her glance to the other side of the room to gather her wits. Geoffrey, meanwhile, took a sip of his wine, yet his eyes never left her face. His attitude had unnerved her, but she should have expected it. Of course, he had invited her to dinner to grill her on AHG operations. She shouldn't have come.

She glanced back at him. The look on his face surprised her; the intensity of the moment before had been replaced with a look of concern. She relaxed her shoulders, still wary of him.

He creased his brows, then said, 'This Ted Branagan, what does he do?'

She felt her defenses rising again. 'What do you mean, what does he do? His job is none of your business.' She was snapping now and didn't like her tone. What had happened to the cool professional she thought she was?

Geoffrey shrugged. 'I just wondered if you were self-directed or if Branagan tells you what to do.'

Susan merely frowned at him, refusing to answer, unsure of his motives.

His features relaxed, though, as he attempted to explain. His voice was softer now. 'I'm sorry if I sounded harsh, Susan. Believe me, I'm all for what you're trying to do. But I'm afraid of the repercussions of some of your investigations.'

'Congressman Winston,' she said, 'if you're here to frighten us out of a commitment to seeing justice applied where it has not been previously, then you won't succeed. Believe me, we're not just a bunch of kids, still wet behind the ears.' If there was anything she hated, it was having the AHG accused of not knowing what it was doing.

He let her finish, then replied with a calmness that somehow riled her even further. 'I didn't mean to imply that you were. I want what's best for you, no matter what you may think. It's just that even the most experienced professionals sometimes have a rough time of it when they come up against government corruption.'

She let down her defenses just slightly at what seemed to be genuine concern in his eyes and she replied, 'I know, and we're helping some of them.'

The waiter returned, and they both looked sheepishly at their menus. Geoffrey said, 'I think we need a little more time.'

'Fine,' said the young man, who then left them alone once more. As they picked up the large stiff menus, the print swam before Susan's eyes. She didn't really care what she ate. But then reason returned, and she settled on halibut, while Geoffrey ordered a sirloin steak.

After the waiter returned and took their order, Geoffrey turned his eyes on her again. His half smile failed to charm her, though.

'Tell you what. Let's not discuss it over dinner. It'll spoil our appetites.'

Susan still felt wary. But she realized she should rein in her thoughts. If they could enjoy a quiet meal, perhaps the discussion later would be more fruitful. If she handled him properly, she might even gain his favor, which would be a big help when it came time for the hearings. After all, the point of the hearing was to get the subcommittees to recommend that Congress take action. If Geoffrey Winston was prejudiced against the AHG, they would have less chance of getting the subcommittee's support. She would bide her time, try to pick up a few clues about his personality, and then give him a few impressive thoughts to chew on.

Pea soup was served, and they dipped into it, crunching their croutons, giving her time to get the conversation on a friendly footing again.

'What about you, Congressman? You haven't told me anything about yourself, and my research hasn't taken me far.' She couldn't keep the irony out of her voice.

He appreciated her small joke, knowing that she most likely would look into the backgrounds of all the subcommittee members the AHG would appear before. 'You know I'm from New Mexico,' he said.

'Yes, but were you born there?'

'Born and raised. My parents live in Silver City.'

'Oh, I know the place,' she said, surprised. 'I'm from Texas myself, and we used to go to the Gila Wilderness for some of our vacations.'

He grinned. 'We always used to complain

about those Texans coming over our mountains to escape the summer heat.'

For a while they talked about their native states, and Susan got him to tell her a little about his home. Aside from his parents, though, he mentioned no one else. She became more curious about his marital status, until she was tempted to ask him outright, but he saved her from questioning him.

'I'm divorced,' he said as he was telling her about Christmas in Albuquerque with his brother's family. 'My ex-wife and two sons live in California now.'

'Oh, I see,' she said, a feeling of relief inexplicably sweeping through her. He didn't seem to mind discussing it.

'I miss the boys, but they come to see me for two weeks at the beginning of summer or before school starts in the fall, and I go to see them when I get a chance.'

'Oh.' She blushed, ashamed of wondering what sort of relationship he had with his wife when he visited his family. She had to warn herself again about getting too personal with this man.

'We're friends,' he said quietly, causing Susan to look up quickly. For a second time she was afraid he could actually see her thoughts as he held her eyes with his, but he described the situation casually, as if it were just a part of the ongoing conversation. Of course, as a politician he had learned to put people at ease, she warned herself.

By the time the main course arrived, she was listening to his anecdotes and descriptions of New Mexico. She remembered the smell of juniper and ponderosa pine on the slopes of the Black Range, and she thought of the mountain lakes and streams her family had camped beside numerous times. She recalled what it was like to lie on a blanket of pine needles and look at the blue sky above.

'How refreshing that must be,' she finally said, much of her earlier antagonism dissipated. 'I haven't had that kind of relaxation for years.'

'Too much work?' he asked.

She frowned, but it wasn't a frown of anger now. He had lightened their conversation considerably, and she could feel that his question had to do with her life-style as a person; it wasn't a gibe at the type of work she did. She even admitted he might be right. 'While I was working at the Library of Congress, I earned my graduate degree in library science. Then I went to work for the AHG. I guess I should take a vacation once in a while.'

'I wish,' he said, moving his hand to pick

up his wineglass but letting his fingers brush her hand, 'that I could show you some of my favorite places in the mountains.'

The wistfulness in his eyes and the resonance of his voice caused a tremor in her, but she could think of no fitting reply, certainly not the one she'd been about to give. *That would be nice*, she wanted to say, but she dared not.

The restaurant was quiet, and the ambience conducive to intimacy. Susan was getting too relaxed, she knew, for the outside world seemed very far away, and she spoke of whatever came to mind — her life, her family in Texas — finally even turning quite naturally to the AHG. She had launched into a description of their recent success reinstating pilots who had lost their licenses because of a conspiracy, when she faltered.

He was watching her intently. In fact, he was such a good listener that she forgot she needed to be wary of him. She forgot what she was saying and looked down at her food, noticing a piece of broccoli that had somehow fallen halfway off her plate.

'Go on,' he prompted her, and this time he did reach across to touch the hand that limply held her fork. 'I am interested.'

Suddenly, a feeling of frustration overcame her. 'Are you?' Her tone held more resentment than she had intended. 'Or are you just trying to trip me up? Form an opinion before we have a chance to state our facts clearly and with documentation?' *Or do you have other, more questionable motives for pumping information out of me,* she wondered.

'No,' he said, anger and surprise mingling. 'You misunderstand me.'

'Do I?' Disappointment washed through her. How silly of her to forget who this man was. It annoyed her that she found him so attractive. His easygoing narratives had woven a spell around her, and she had fallen for it. But she was on her guard now — wary of a trap.

Still, when she looked into his brown eyes, she felt confusion. He was so convincing. As he took her hand in his, she could feel his strength and determination.

'Susan, I'm sorry. You misunderstand my intentions. I am not trying anything under-handed concerning the AHG. I am simply interested. And — ' his gaze swept over her face and hair, briefly taking in her shoulders and neckline ' — I enjoy your company.'

'Yes, I know,' she said, her breathing more shallow. His quick glance over her told her what her inner instincts were responding to. He was as attracted to her as she was to him.

His grip on her hand, his look, the signals that passed between them, were unmistakable. She dropped her gaze, not knowing what to say. How dare he do this to her? He was probably using his charm to get information out of her. Wasn't he?

Geoffrey called for the check, and Susan fiddled with her napkin. They hadn't ordered dessert, and so she assumed Geoffrey might suggest going somewhere else for coffee or an aperitif. It would give her a chance to gather her wits, try to find out what it was he wanted. Neither of them spoke as he settled the bill.

On the sidewalk, Geoffrey touched his hand to her waist and held her gently as they walked along. Night had fallen. Her hair accidentally brushed his cheek, and he turned his face slightly toward her, breathing in her perfume. A tremor within her began as he matched his step to hers, his hand guiding her in and out of the crowd.

'Would you like to get a cup of coffee at the park?' Geoffrey asked.

'That would be fine,' she said in a low voice. *Look out,* a voice in her head told her. *He's coming on too strong.* Yet she could not get over her own responses to him. She felt comfortable in his presence, and her body seemed to crave his nearness. *You're playing with fire*, the voice said.

Please, another voice answered. *A harmless kiss, perhaps?* At the thought of his mouth on hers, a spring in the core of her seemed to explode. She knew that if he wanted to kiss her, she would crave his embrace. For ideologies could not stand in the way when that special spark between a man and a woman was ignited. She swallowed hard, willing her unruly desires to be stilled.

They turned into the arcade that housed three floors of shops, restaurants and art galleries. Georgetown Park was a popular place built in tiers, open to an atrium two levels down from the ground-floor entrance. The structure was built into the hill that led down to the Potomac. Inside, an elevator carried people between the tiers of establishments, but Geoffrey and Susan walked slowly next to the railing until they came to the stairs. On the lower floor a din of voices from several eating places provided a neutral background.

The lights and colorful window displays helped her slow down her rushing blood. She tried to think of the way Ted would handle Geoffrey Winston and the clever way in which Ted was always able to contrive a conversation so that the other person would wind up revealing more than he'd meant. But Susan felt tongue-tied. She didn't seem to have the same talent.

They threaded their way through a crowd of families to a coffee bar.

'I don't really want dessert, do you?' she asked him.

'Coffee is fine with me,' he said.

'Then let's just get two cups and sit out here.' She indicated the benches next to some greenery surrounding a fountain where they could sit and watch the crowds.

He stepped up and ordered two cups of coffee, inquiring how she liked hers.

'Light, no sugar,' she said.

Then she took the paper cup, letting the warmth seep into her hands. They sat down together, and he moved close enough to brush her arm but not to cramp her. She smiled, watching the crowds go by, among them couples young and old, some with children trailing behind. It reminded her that Geoffrey had children.

'How old are your sons?' she asked, trying to envision a small tot with some of Geoffrey's features and not succeeding very well.

He said nothing until she turned to look at him to find out why he hesitated to answer her. He was grinning from ear to ear. 'Sixteen and twenty,' he said.

She smiled. 'But you don't look that — '

'Old?'

Her eyes widened, and her face turned red. 'What an awful thing to say,' she replied. 'I'm sorry.'

But he was amused by her embarrassment. 'It's all right. I'm not hiding my age. I'm forty-two.' He leaned forward, resting his elbows on his thighs, holding the coffee in front of him.

She did a quick calculation as he watched her.

'I met Marilyn while we were still in college,' he said. 'We got married just before graduation. I worked for three years; then Marilyn returned to work and put me through law school.'

'It must have been a struggle with a child so young.'

His face darkened as he sipped his coffee. 'It wasn't planned to be that way, but you do the best you can.'

'Oh.' She looked down. She hadn't meant to delve into his personal life, and yet she was flattered that he would tell her.

'It's all right,' he said. 'I don't mind telling you about it. And I regret nothing. Our sons have brought us both joy.' He smiled lopsidedly at her. 'You'd like them.'

Again her eyes widened as she thought of

two tall teenagers. Why, the elder was only nine years younger than she was.

His eyes took on that soft, vulnerable look again as he said, 'They'd like you, too.'

'Your ex-wife,' Susan said, turning to look ahead at the passersby. 'What is she like?'

'She's a good person. We're very good friends. But when you marry that young, a lot can happen as you grow older, and you want to explore. She had no interest in politics, and I can understand why. The campaign trail can be a burden. So we parted friends. She's remarried.'

'Oh.' This time she said it with surprise. She realized she had gotten the answer to an earlier question she'd had.

Geoffrey seemed to be appraising her as if he knew that his explanations were saying more than just the spoken words. He seemed to sense her questions and was answering them.

Susan glanced over at him, from the strong hands that held the coffee cup, to the elbows resting on his thighs, to the wavy hair. Again she was moved by his openness, in spite of herself. Perhaps she had misjudged him at first. Still, she didn't dare trust him. He had badgered her about the AHG at dinner. And it wouldn't do to allow a rumor to start about them. Washington loved gossip, and while she had never seen her own name in the papers except in connection with AHG news, she knew that there were those who eagerly followed the doings of congressmen and whom they were seen with in public. And she and Geoffrey were certainly in public now.

No, she thought, pressing her lips together. It wouldn't do.

'Come on,' said Geoffrey, crushing his cup and rising in one motion. He reached for her hand, and she followed him across the tiled floor to deposit their cups in a garbage can. 'Let's get some fresh air.'

She nodded. They mounted the steps and found their way to the street-level exit again. They crossed Prospect Street and walked up Potomac Street. The sound of traffic was gradually replaced by footsteps on the brick sidewalk and individual voices as people drifted by. Geoffrey again held her waist, his arm against her shoulder. They walked in silence as they breathed the crisp night air. When the wind was right, they could smell the scent of the Potomac River behind them, below the slopes of Georgetown. They had gone several blocks when Susan realized he had left his car behind. 'Your car,' she began.

'Where do you live?' he interrupted, waving away concern about his car.

'P Street.'

'I'll walk you home, then get my car,' he said.

The streetlights — old gas lamps that had been converted to electricity — cast a mellow glow over sections of the street, leaving most of the sidewalk in intimate obscurity. They walked through the darkness, a light chill still holding the air. In a few weeks the cherry blossoms would bloom, and the air would be full of the intoxicating scents of a myriad of flowers. But it was still too early for that. Winter retained a determined hold as it blew the last of its breaths over the city.

'It must be warm now in New Mexico,' she said, her own voice jarring her out of the cocoon of silence that had formed around them.

'Oh, yes,' he said. 'You should see the sunrise on an early spring morning in the West.'

She could imagine the rivers rushing along, full with melting snow from the mountain heights. Even the desert floor would be full of life as animals and plants carried out their business. What a world — so far from the granite and marble of Washington.

'Left here,' she said as they reached O Street and broke their stride to cross the street. They continued past the cozy town houses, warm lights glimmering inside many

56

of them, and turned on Thirty-fifth Street, walking toward P Street. She felt a little flutter as they approached the red brick town house with neat white shutters. She reached in her pocket for the keys. She would have to get her briefcase out of the car tomorrow, she remembered. There was nothing confidential in it, so she didn't need to worry about that now. They stepped up to the porch.

Looking at Geoffrey, she felt hesitant. She hated to say good-night in spite of her doubts about him. If only . . .

He turned her head by placing a finger under her chin, and though it was dark, she could see the light in his eyes, feel his breath warming her mouth. 'I've enjoyed it,' he said.

'So — ' But she never finished, for his right arm went around her back, and his mouth found hers. Her senses spun as he kissed her. She relaxed her lips against his, letting him support her back with his strong arms.

His kiss continued, and her lips parted, welcoming his mouth. A thrill began low in her body, sending heat through her veins. She didn't remember ever enjoying a kiss so much. She yearned for more as his hands found their way under her jacket, moving slowly across the back of her shirt.

He was bending her backward slightly, pulling the lower part of her body closer to his. A shock rippled through her as his mouth left hers to explore her earlobe and neck. At the same time, he moved his body ever so slightly, so that her thigh came between his legs and she felt the hardness of him beneath his clothes.

She had a nearly uncontrollable urge to move herself against him but resisted, raking one hand through his hair and massaging his back with her other hand. *Yes,* her womanly body cried out. *More,* her senses said. *It was crazy,* some frightened part of her cautioned, to behave like this with a man on her doorstep; a man who probably wanted a great deal more from her than this.

The situation posed a threat to the AHG. That rang bells in her head and stemmed the tide that was racing through her, threatening to engulf them both. As much as she was tempted by Geoffrey Winston the man, she could not forget that he was a congressman and could do much to help or hinder the cause she was most committed to.

She used both hands to press back his shoulders, turning her face away from him as she said, 'I don't think I'd better ask you in.'

He eased her out of the hold he had on her but kept her within reach of his lips, placing small kisses on her forehead and hair. 'May I see you again?' he asked. The huskiness of his tone touched her.

'I'd like that,' she said in a low voice, taking a breath to try to control her rioting senses.

'Tomorrow?'

'Tomorrow? Isn't that too soon?' She looked about as if the environment could somehow provide an answer. But only the quaking branches and the purr of a car at the far end of the block answered her. She hadn't had time to think about tomorrow. 'Tomorrow?' she said again.

He studied her. 'I want to see you again soon. Before you build up some prejudice against me,' he said.

She exhaled a breath. What did that mean? He wanted to see her again while she was still under his undeniable influence?

He traced the hollow of her cheek with his finger. 'Look, I didn't mean to do that just now. I thought we would just talk. But ... you're beautiful, Susan.' His brows knotted. That didn't really express his feelings for her. It was more than that. He sensed her intellectual depth, and they shared a common interest. If only he could persuade her to cooperate with him. Instead, he said, 'I don't want to give you the wrong idea about me.'

At that moment Susan was unsure of just what the right idea was. She didn't want it to end like this, either, though. Not with both of them struggling for words and feeling unsatisfied. She thought quickly. Tomorrow really was too soon. She would have to see Ted, go over today's research — form a battle plan for the coming week. That was something they always did away from the office, before the hectic routine of the week began.

'I really can't,' she said, trying to sound firm. Besides, she needed a day to think this out — let Ted know she had met the congressman. Avoid rumors.

'Call me during the week.' She reached into her pocketbook for the business cards she always carried there for times when she was without her briefcase.

He took the card and looked at it. Then he looked at her. 'Do you mind,' he said slowly, 'if I call you at home instead of at your office?'

'Why . . . ' Her heart hammered. Obviously he had some reason why he didn't want her colleagues at the AHG to know he was seeing her. She knew she was taking a chance, but . . . 'All right,' she said. She didn't look at him as she dug for a pen to scribble her home number on the card, deciding that she would play the game if he wanted to talk to her again. She was still determined to find out what he wanted. 'Do you have something to write with?' she asked.

He reached into his breast pocket and extracted a silver pen with a small digital clock on one end. She took it and placed her card against the door to write her home phone number on the back of it. A flash of guilt assailed her, but biting her lip as she wrote, she promised herself she would turn the relationship to good advantage for the AHG's causes.

'I'll call you at home, then,' he said. 'Thank you again for having dinner with me,' he said, pocketing the pen and the card. He gazed at her, and confusing emotions again assailed her. She knew another kiss would be dangerous.

She turned. 'It was a pleasure,' she said, unlocking the door and pushing it in.

He gazed at the town house. 'Which floor do you live on?' he asked.

'Second,' she said, one foot on the doorsill. 'The owners live in the front and side of the downstairs and rent a small apartment to a German student in the back. I have the upstairs. A bedroom, sitting room, kitchen and bath. It's comfortable.'

He nodded, stepping back down to the sidewalk and looking up as if envisioning her apartment while he looked at her shuttered windows. 'Very nice, these old houses. A real flavor, and built to last.'

'Umm,' she said, stepping all the way in. 'I'll talk to you this week then . . . Geoffrey.' It was the first time she had addressed him by his first name. 'Good night,' she said in a softer tone.

'Good night' came his deep voice. Then she listened to the sound of his footsteps on the sidewalk as he walked away. It still bothered her that he'd asked for her home phone number, but she didn't want to think about it anymore tonight.

Across the street, the light-haired man with the red scar under his eye came out of a door and walked down the stoop, tossing a cigarette into the street. Susan noticed him as she was about to close the door. He looked up, saw her watching him, and nodded slightly before he turned to walk up the street.

Oh, thought Susan, *he must have rented an apartment in the house across the street.* She remembered the maroon Toyota from the other day. She shrugged and went in. Since they were so near the university, people were always moving in and out along here. She wondered if she'd meet him sometime.

3

Sunday night Susan and Ted sat on cushions around a low coffee table in front of Ted's blue-and-green-striped sofa. They had just finished a pizza and were discussing their strategy for the week. She had tried to think of a way to tell Ted about Geoffrey Winston. Finally, while Ted was digesting the last bite of whole wheat pizza, she said, 'I ran into Congressman Winston at the National Archives yesterday.'

'Oh,' Ted said, taking a sip of soda to wash down the pizza. He leaned back on the sofa and stretched out his legs in front of him, bits of material torn out of the hem of his jeans as if a dog had chewed on them. The remains of the pizza were strewn in a cardboard container on the sturdy wooden coffee table. Susan began to gather up their garbage as she spoke.

'What was he doing there?' Ted asked. 'Did you talk to him?'

Susan avoided his glance. 'Yes. He recognized me, and we left the building together.'

'Not prying information out of you about

our hearing, I hope?'

She looked away. 'No. He didn't ask me about the cases we're handling . . . directly.'

Ted frowned and paid more attention. 'What do you mean, directly? Did he want to know something else?'

A picture flashed through her mind of Geoffrey bending her over backward on her porch and arousing her passion with a kiss. 'Well, he did want to know a little about us.'

Ted gathered his feet under him and hiked himself up straighter against his end of the sofa. 'Susan, I think you'd better tell me about this. It could be important.'

She shrugged, trying to sound nonchalant. 'Just in a friendly sort of way, you know. Oh, Ted,' she tried to tease him, 'don't scowl. He's just interested, that's all.'

'What did he say, specifically?'

'It's hard to remember. He asked how I had come to work for the AHG. He did caution us about getting in over our heads.'

Ted scrambled forward, his face dark with anger, his cheekbones looking more prominent, heightening his look of intensity. 'What did he mean by that? Does he think we don't know what we're doing, or was it a threat? Susan, you may not be aware of it, but it's important that you tell me exactly what he said — exactly.'

She said in a low voice, 'I know. I asked him that, too — if he was threatening us. He said no, but that he was afraid we would run into trouble with some of our cases if we bumped into a nest of people who really have something big to hide.'

Ted was silent, but as Susan watched him, she could see the turbulence that lay behind his expression. Then he said, 'I wonder if he has a reason for steering us away from something. You say he didn't mention any cases specifically.'

'Believe me, Ted, I would have fished for information if I'd thought he had any. I don't think he does.'

But a stab of guilt assailed her. Hadn't there been a gap of time when she hadn't been on her guard — hadn't been thinking about her job at all? Or about the people who came to them in confidence? She felt foolish. If Ted knew about that, he would be furious. She looked up as Ted rose to pace across his worn braid rug.

'Ted, I — I — ' she stuttered, 'don't think there's any reason to be suspicious.' But she knew it sounded lame. If she were Ted, she would have seized such an opportunity alone with the congressman to pick his brain and try to assess what he was up to. But she hadn't done that, she thought with a shudder.

She had fallen for Geoffrey's masculine charm, and she had dropped her vigilance. She had failed.

She tried to mask her distress by busying herself with the soda cans and straws, but Ted stopped, legs spread, looking down at her where she knelt on the floor.

'I hope you can avoid running into him again,' he said, 'unless you can trust yourself to keep your mouth shut about our business.'

That hurt. 'Ted,' she protested, looking up at him as he seemed to take the pose of interrogator, 'you know I never break security. Besides, what's so secret, anyway? The worst that could happen is that one of us could spill a rumor that hasn't yet been documented. This isn't espionage, you know.'

'No, but we do guarantee confidentiality to people who come to us.'

'Oh, Ted, don't worry. I don't even remember those people's names. My job is just to dig up government facts. You know that.'

'You sound as if you're planning to see him again.'

'Well — ' she shrugged, curling a lock of hair in her fingers ' — he did ask me if he could call me.'

Ted took a step toward her. 'He did what?'

'Uh, yeah. We might have lunch or something.'

Suddenly, two iron hands gripped her shoulders and lifted her to her feet. She dropped the empty soda cans to the floor with a clatter as she found herself staring into Ted's flashing green eyes. A muscle twitched under his left eye, and his lips formed a hard line.

'What's going on, Susan? Do I detect some feminine interest in this man? Have you ever met him before?'

Susan gasped for breath and stared back into the hard, glinting eyes. 'I can't answer you if you ask me so many questions all at once. Now what is it you want to know? One question at a time, please.'

He let go of her shoulders, and she rubbed the right one with her left hand, afraid he had left a bruise, but she continued to meet his glare with one of her own, though her heart was hammering. *Ted may have an Irish temper,* she thought, *but I'm not about to stand here and be abused.*

Then she turned away from him, quelling her own anger. Fighting over the issue would do no good. She originated the answers he wanted to know. 'I'd never met him before. After that press conference he dropped into, I went to the newspaper-clip files and got a little background data. When we met at the archives, he seemed very nice, said he wanted to talk to me, so we went to have something to eat.'

'You *what*?'

But she raised a palm in front of her to stop another tirade from breaking out. 'If you want to know, I do think he's attractive. Not everything we talked about was political.' She glowered at Ted, daring him to shout her down again.

But Ted merely scratched the back of his head in an agitated manner.

'Ted, what harm is there in it? I'm not going to divulge any trade secrets.'

'But the press — '

'The press isn't going to know about it. It's not as if we're having a clandestine affair.' Even as she said it, she felt the heat rising in her veins.

He sighed, bringing his annoyance under control with obvious effort. Then his expression relaxed, and he seemed to take another tack.

'Susan, I — ' he hesitated ' — I guess it was a surprise to hear of your having dinner with him.' He shrugged, then threw himself down again, his thumbs hooked into the belt loops of his blue jeans. 'We spend so much time together, you and I. It's just, you know

. . . Well, I didn't know you had time for anything else. Anyone else,' he amended, frowning straight ahead.

'Ted,' she said, her voice incredulous, 'you don't mean you're — ' she didn't know how to put it. Ted jealous? But they weren't even lovers. 'Well, you know it doesn't mean anything,' she continued. It sounded silly to try to convince Ted that her seeing Geoffrey Winston had nothing to do with her friendship with Ted. It didn't seem to at the moment, but suddenly she felt as if she were walking on shifting sands and didn't know where the wind would blow her next.

After a feeble attempt at reducing the strain between them, they went over reports sent in from the chapters of the AHG around the country. More people had come to their interviewers complaining of harassment from law enforcement agencies. Many claimed to know of false reports being circulated about them and were having difficulty clearing their records even after they'd been proved innocent. One citizen they had talked to had been taken into custody on suspicion of burglary. He had done nothing wrong, but he had been in the same neighborhood where a prowler had been reported. Later the burglar was caught, but the original suspect's record remained in police files.

Finally, they finished, and Susan stood up to go. Ted ran his fingers through his dark hair, and she watched the curls spring back into place after his hand passed through them. His eyes still carried a hurt look, making Susan feel as if she had betrayed him. She tried to smooth his ruffled feathers, but she drove home feeling uneasy.

She had had disagreements with Ted before but never one that seemed to touch so many sore spots as this one had. On the one hand, she felt guilty about her interest in a member of a subcommittee to whom she would soon be presenting evidence. It smacked of underhandedness. But she also felt angry that Ted should think he could tell her what to do with her life. His attitude rankled her. She should at least have the right to make the decision herself.

★ ★ ★

Ted had been closeted for quite a while with the man who had come for an interview. Ted was handling this interview himself because Tammy and Michael were tied up. Susan also suspected that he had a special interest in the issue of false reports and wanted a hand in interviewing those who came to them with complaints. That false reports about private citizens were being circulated among law enforcement agencies was certain. Individuals arrested but not convicted remained in law enforcement agency files long after the real criminal was found. A pattern was forming. It was almost as if someone were cluttering up the data base of suspects to draw suspicion away from bigger crimes.

But that was only a theory that Susan and Ted had come up with last night. And she realized this morning, as she filled out reports on her desk, that she was anxious to know what Ted had learned from the morning's interview. Ted had been talking for nearly an hour to the man who had come in. How much longer would they be cloistered in the interview room, she wondered.

She was tired of her paperwork, so she stood up, stretched and walked over to the coffee maker at the side of the room. The pot held the dregs of this morning's coffee, so she decided to make a fresh pot.

As she was placing a new packet of coffee grounds in the filter, Tammy came through the door.

'Hi,' Susan said.

'Hi,' returned the redheaded interviewer. She handed Susan a piece of paper. 'It seems these state and local police agencies exchange information via Globenet.' Susan and Tammy had already discussed the function of the international network of police forces in distributing information on criminal suspects, and Tammy brought Susan any data she had on Globenet's possible connection with false reports. 'Twenty thousand of them,' Tammy continued.

Susan nodded.

'Why don't you find out how the information is sent? Is there a central computer? And who okays the info that's distributed? Seems to me these false reports might be slipping through Globenet's fingers as a result of too few checks and balances.'

'I see,' said Susan. 'I'll look into it.' She inserted the coffee filter in the coffee maker.

Just then the door opened, and a middle-aged man with heavy jowls and thinning hair appeared. He turned and shook hands with Ted, who followed him out, muttered a few words, then looked around the room, not knowing which way was out. Ted ushered him past the gray metal desks to the front door, thanking him for coming in. After the man passed through, Ted ran his fingers through his thick, dark hair and swung around. He smiled at Susan and Tammy, and they looked at him expectantly.

'More evidence of false reports,' he said. 'The assistant manager of an appliance store in New York. On his way out of the store last year, he was arrested. The police checked his driver's license with the FBI's computer at the National Crime Information Center. According to the readout, he was a wanted criminal. He was taken to New York's Seventeenth Precinct and booked. He spent eleven days in jail before the police learned there had been a mix-up.'

'Didn't they check his fingerprints?'

'He asked them to, but they didn't believe his protestations of innocence because the identification numbers matched. Programmers at the National Crime Information Center in Washington had incorrectly combined data from his file with that of another man of the same name.'

Susan shook her head. Similar incidents had occurred both in the United States and in Canada. 'It makes the police who handle these cases look like a bunch of idiots.'

Ted raised a dark brow. 'Perhaps someone intends it to look that way.'

They had discussed that possibility last night. In cases like this, it took weeks, sometimes months, to straighten out the confusion. One of their other clients with a similar problem with false information had commented that 'the information in the computer is only as good as the person putting it in or taking it out.' That may explain the mix-ups, but it didn't excuse the injustices done to the victims of the blunderers — if indeed these were only errors.

Ted thought it went further than that. Somebody, somewhere, was actually pulling strings to circulate false reports about private citizens, whether they were innocent or guilty of petty crimes such as traffic violations. The AHG's job was to find out who was controlling the data and why, then bring the evidence before the congressional subcommittee.

Susan became thoughtful as she returned to her desk. There were half a million computerized 'criminal' histories in the NCIC computer, and if a person ever had significant contact with a local or federal law enforcement agency, there was a record of it. That the record might not be accurate, that it might be mixed up with that of some other less reputable person, was a chilling possibility. It might be the report of a mistaken arrest, or it might tell only half the story if the records were not removed if the person was later found innocent of charges.

Susan had just that morning read a quoted remark by the chairman of a senate subcommittee on constitutional rights. 'An incredible seventy percent of all arrest records in the United States do not include final disposition of the case.'

She buried herself in work for the rest of the day, and at six o'clock she drove home and trudged up the stairs to her apartment, feeling out of sorts. Though she and Ted made no further mention of Geoffrey Winston after last night, Susan felt uncomfortable about the situation. Perhaps the best thing to do would be not to see Geoffrey again. Besides, he might not even call her. Their dinner together might have been nothing more than a hiatus in otherwise routine lives they had set for themselves — a romantic encounter caused by a chance meeting.

Her heart gave a little flutter as she turned the lock in her door. Inside, she dropped her things on the sofa and pushed the door shut behind her, locking it. Then she turned on the lamp and went to look out the window. The days were getting longer now, and at six o'clock dusk was just beginning to erase the shadows of leaves that had danced on the bricked street all afternoon. Across the street a woman stood on her porch talking to a man who was leaning on a car parked at the curb under a tall elm.

Susan turned back into the room and gave

a little frown. Though nothing upsetting had actually happened today, she had the odd feeling that things on the fringes of her life didn't quite add up just now. Why had Ted been so angry about Geoffrey? At first, it had seemed that he was afraid of Geoffrey's being a snoop. But when Susan had told him she thought that unlikely, he had almost reverted to a plea of jealousy, which made no sense. He didn't own Susan and had never made any advances toward her.

And Geoffrey Winston himself was a puzzle, as well. Why had he become interested in Susan? Did he have some ulterior motive in finding out what the AHG was doing? Was he planning to use her in some way?

She squeezed her arms, which were crossed in front of her chest. She had been foolish to fall victim to the congressman's advances. She would not let it happen again. But even as she said it, a sliver of doubt forced its way into her thoughts. When she saw him again, would she be able to keep her encounter with him on a business footing? She remembered those soft brown eyes that seemed to engulf her in his look, his big strong hands on her back, his thighs against hers, and she trembled.

Then she let go of her arms and pulled the

drapes shut, for soon it would be dark. She turned on the lamp over her worktable and fetched her briefcase. Clearing a space, she sat down and extracted the photocopies she had made of some news stories she had read that day. She had done no further research on Geoffrey Winston. It had not been a conscious decision, but perhaps she had to keep her thinking clear by avoiding him altogether as a subject of her research. Instead, she had details on the backgrounds and interests of the other subcommittee members.

She pulled out several photocopies and adjusted the light. The face on the top sheet, blurred from the photocopy, stared off the page in a forced smile. This was Irwin Bradshaw. He looked familiar to her. She'd probably seen him in the papers before. He was a Democrat from Louisiana, and in this photo he was shaking hands with an administrator from the Environmental Protection Agency. Even in the blurry photo, Susan could see the hard-looking eyes. The thin smile did not reach his eyes.

Then she dropped the paper. *Oh, stop it*, she told herself. Everything was suddenly becoming suspicious. She took a slow breath and exhaled. She never used to be this way. Was it her job at the AHG that made her analyze everything she saw? She seemed to be looking deeper than she used to behind people's façades, looking for ulterior motives.

She shook her head. The gnaw of hunger in her stomach reminded her it was past six o'clock. As she went to hunt through the refrigerator for something edible, she reflected on the effect her job had had on her. She had been so busy with it and so hyped on its purpose that she hadn't taken a close look at her own life in some time. A bit of introspection might not hurt.

As she prepared a ham-and-cheese sandwich on whole wheat bread, she thought about her reasons for joining the AHG. She began to recall how it had been when she had first met Ted. A picture of the poster that had first attracted her flew into her mind. It was a print of a pen-and-ink drawing of Uncle Sam pointing a finger. 'Honesty Pays . . . ' it said. Then it went on to announce that the AHG would pay up to ten thousand dollars for information about government officials leading to their arrest and conviction for corruption in office. Bribery, extortion, harboring criminals, failure to report a crime, theft, conspiracy to commit a felony, discriminatory prosecution or other instances of crimes — she rattled off the litany she had repeated dozens of times since then.

And they had gotten responses, too. Ted had led a campaign to open up chapters of the AHG in twenty cities throughout the United States. And when she thought of the number of crimes the AHG investigators had uncovered, combined with the number of people who had come to them of their own volition, she had to stop and stare into space. She had gotten back to the table and put her plate with the sandwich down by Irwin Bradshaw's picture. Then she got up again to return for the mayonnaise and a knife. She never put enough mayo on her sandwiches.

Images of some of their early cases passed through her mind. She remembered the man who had come to the AHG last fall with documents proving that highly confidential White House and Pentagon communiqués were being leaked. He felt that the security leaks might have caused the deaths of American soldiers in Vietnam, but when he had tried to blow the whistle in 1973, he was warned to keep quiet if he knew which side his bread was buttered on. The AHG helped the man with his case by doing further investigation into the Saigon security leaks. The information they uncovered was passed on to interested members of Congress.

Then Susan's hand stopped midair as her mouth opened for a bite of the sandwich.

Irwin Bradshaw, she remembered, had been one of the congressmen who had expressed interest in that case. She tried to see the picture in her mind more clearly. The small mouth, the small eyes set close together, a long, straight nose. Yes, she did remember him briefly. She hadn't had any real contact with him, but then, she had only taken a background role in that case. She had been new at the AHG, just learning the ropes from Ted. She had been busy studying requests for documents using the Freedom of Information Act. She never would have thought about Irwin Bradshaw again if he hadn't turned up on this congressional subcommittee.

* * *

Geoffrey Winston stared out the window of his apartment on Virginia Avenue. Across the street a modern white high rise towered over small, elegant Georgian houses on either side. Ten floors below him traffic swarmed, but he was oblivious to it. Evening was drawing near, and he had turned on his two Tiffany lamps to dispel the gloom. His living room was comfortably arranged, with a dark brown plush sofa and a matching armchair, an Oriental rug with the same shade of brown in its intricate combination of beiges and greens,

80

and teakwood furniture, all carefully chosen by the interior decorator he had paid a bundle to do the job. And Mrs. Hennessy, his fifty-four-year-old housekeeper, picked up after him. Though she was only twelve years older than he was, she adopted a matronly attitude toward him. Her own sons were gone from home, and she seemed to enjoy keeping house for him, cooking dinners when he wasn't planning on dining out. She left them in the kitchen for him to heat up in the microwave oven whenever his erratic schedule allowed.

He turned from the window, where he had been watching the lights go on in the white monolith across the street. His eye caught the two photographs in dark wooden frames on the piano; the faces seemed to smile at him and made his chest expand. Timothy and Brent would be coming for a visit soon. They had wanted to come to see him at the end of May, before summer jobs claimed them. His moment of happiness carried him as far as the kitchen, where he spied the covered dish with a note from Mrs. Hennessy; then he busied himself arranging the food so it could go into the microwave.

He smiled at the folded linen napkin and silverware Mrs. Hennessy had left. Then he turned on the microwave and returned to the living room to gaze out the window again. This was where he did a lot of thinking.

The darkness outside was taking hold, and the living room began to lose its warmth. His left brow lowered in annoyance as the timer went off, and he returned to the kitchen. He liked his apartment. Of course, it was nothing compared to his sprawling Mexican-style house on the outskirts of Albuquerque. That was where he put his own thought and care into a living space. The Washington apartment was just a hutch to keep him when he was in Washington. And being in politics, he never knew how long that would be.

He carried his dinner to the dining-room table a few feet away from the window and sat down. Then he began to feel depressed. Even the boys' grins from the piano failed to lighten his mood. The olive-colored telephone on its black wrought-iron stand next to his easy chair caught his eye. He had been trying not to think of it. But after he tasted the first delicious bite of Mrs. Hennessy's vegetarian lasagna, his hand fell heavily, the fork clattering on the plate. Saturday evening's dinner with Susan Franks came back to him full force, causing a crushed sensation around his heart. He cast a wistful look at the telephone.

Damn it, he wanted to call her. He wanted

to be with her again. It annoyed him that he was fighting his natural inclinations. He had never had a problem with women. He and his wife had carried out their entire relationship in honesty, muddling through problems together even when they felt ill equipped. When their lives had changed, and when what they both wanted as individuals had changed, they had faced up to it. It had been difficult, of course, to know he was losing someone he had once loved and who had once loved him, but for several years they had lived in the past, for the boys' sake. Then a time had come when they handled the situation as intelligently as possible, and they had gotten a divorce. After that, they had slowly drifted apart, and then Marilyn had met Scott, who was a generous provider, and she had married him.

But where had that left Geoffrey? He glowered at the lasagna. He wasn't a promiscuous man. He wanted a home and a family now. For ten years, politics had swept him away, and he had delved into issues that he thought he could do something about. In a way, the work had saved him. Between campaigning and work in Congress, plus keeping tabs on the needs of his constituents, he hadn't had time to feel lonely. He had sought female companionship when his primal urges forced themselves to the surface and when women had thrown themselves at him. But after Marilyn, he had met no one who seemed to satisfy all his needs. Once his physical desires were taken care of, he was left wanting more, and the women he knew, though able and intelligent for the most part, had not fitted quite right. And so he had made no commitments. He hadn't intended to unless he found a woman who could be committed to the same things he was and wouldn't mind being married to a divorced parent.

Then he saw Susan Franks that day at the AHG's press conference. She was stunning in a quiet way. Her dark hair and dark suit complemented a smooth skin and serious brown eyes. She was a tad too thin, but he suspected that was because she drove herself too hard. *Capable*, that's what he had thought when he saw her across the room. And his male instincts had taken that unmistakable leap. She had seemed more than just a beautiful woman. He knew then he had to get to know her.

Odd, then, that the job he had to do demanded it. In a way that had made the initial contact easier. He remembered her slight shyness when they met at the microfilm desk at the National Archives. That's what he liked about her. Everything about her was understated.

He remembered something else, too — the way she had kept in the background at the press conference, supporting Ted Branagan and yet looking as if she could easily have taken over. The thought of Ted Branagan brought another scowl to Geoffrey's face, and he ground his teeth together. What was the relationship between Ted and Susan, anyway? She hadn't discussed that side of her personal life, but when she had mentioned Ted, Geoffrey had sensed that she had an intense loyalty to him.

That bothered Geoffrey deeply. How much did she know about Ted? Were they on intimate terms? She had briefly mentioned Ted's college years and his travel abroad, but only in generalities. Of course, he couldn't expect Susan to tell him everything about Ted on their first meeting. She would think it was none of his business. But then confusion assailed him, and he pushed back his chair to go to the liquor cabinet, across from the sofa, and pour himself a double whiskey. After being with Susan Franks for only an hour, he knew he wanted her — knew she was the woman he had been looking for to fill the void in his life. Surely she sensed it, too. He had made no effort to mask his emotions.

He simply hadn't verbalized his thoughts. But his eyes had said it. His hands and his body had said it as he'd held her.

He recalled with pleasure the way she had felt while pressed against him; so soft and pliable, even though there was an inner strength that could see her through the greatest difficulties. He sighed, then tilted his glass against his lips. The warmth flooding his body drained away as he concentrated on what those difficulties might be. As he organized his thoughts, he opened the cabinet to his stereo. Playing classical music always helped him to think. He chose *The Four Seasons*. The precise, clean tones of Vivaldi were stimulating.

He looked at his whiskey glass but decided to make coffee instead. He would call Susan tonight, he decided impulsively. His hands shook a little as fear threatened him. Could she really be in danger? He knew the AHG was getting close to the source of the false reports to law enforcement agencies, and he was afraid of what might happen when they got too close.

Thank heavens it wasn't an election year. He had never been a man to compromise, but he couldn't help being affected by the caution a politician found necessary before an election. He either had to make promises he thought could be kept, or rush around expediting projects that looked as if they were close to bringing the results he needed, so that he would look as good to his constituents as he believed he was.

He sighed. It had been that sort of thing that had driven Marilyn crazy. He had never doubted himself, but Marilyn had not trusted political tactics. And she was too quiet a person to enjoy the limelight much. He was glad she was with Scott now — a reliable architect who would take good care of the family.

His thoughts returned to Susan. She was already in the thick of it. He could sense her drive and dedication. The warm feeling returned again, and as he thought of his lips in her hair, he recalled the faint trace of her perfume. His body began to ache with desire again, and he decided to call her. He sat down in the easy chair and picked up the card he had placed on the telephone stand. His hand paused on the telephone. He half smiled at his own hesitancy. He was like a young man courting again — worried about her reaction to him, not wanting to come on too strong. Then a worry line creased his brow as he realized he didn't want to frighten her with his intentions, either.

⋆ ⋆ ⋆

The ringing of the phone startled Susan from her work. Even though she had turned the bell down, it never failed to make her jump. She really didn't like telephones; they were always interfering with a person's thoughts or interrupting one's conversations with others.

'Hello,' she said.

The low, deep voice caressed her ear. 'Hello, Susan. This is Geoffrey Winston.'

For a shocked moment she felt breathless. He had said he would call, and yet now that he had, she felt caught off guard; uncertain how to handle it. To break the awkward silence, she said, 'Yes, hello. I — I didn't expect you to call so soon.'

'No?' A brief silence. 'I was thinking about you. I just finished a lonely dinner.' He tried to make it sound like a lighthearted joke about his divorced status, but it came out sounding pitiful.

She could hear the sincerity in his voice. 'Oh? That's nice — that you were thinking about me, I mean.' Her comment had made it sound as if she thought it was nice that he had lonely dinners.

Suddenly she sighed and dropped all pretense of trying to make everything sound right. 'I'm glad you called,' she said.

'I'd like to see you.'

'Yes, I think we should talk.'

'Good. When are you free?' he asked.

'How about Sunday?'

'Fine.' His voice rose in enthusiasm. 'Let's take a drive, see something historical. There's nothing like a historic setting to relax and inspire me.'

'All right. I like your originality.'

'Why don't we drive down to Williamsburg? We could leave early. We'd have time to drive down, time to walk around the town and have a relaxed dinner at the inn.'

Susan's chest contracted at the idea of a romantic dinner at an inn. But there was one advantage to his idea. It was two and a half hours from Washington. They might be afforded more privacy than they would find if they stayed in town, and the change of environment might help them sort out their thoughts. Yes, it was a nice idea. Williamsburg would be an ideal setting in which she could get to know Geoffrey Winston better.

'What time shall I be ready?'

4

Susan glanced out the window as she tugged on her taupe-colored knee-high stocking. Blasted stocking didn't stretch as high on her calf as the one on the other leg. She was always losing the mates, but these would just have to do, for Geoffrey would be there in five minutes. She smoothed down her wool pant leg and stepped into her brown loafers.

She gave a final brush to her hair. It was glossy clean, the soft brown-and-burgundy tweed she wore bringing out the dark brown sheen. She checked her makeup, making sure there was no telltale line under her chin. Then she glanced around the apartment, anxiety nagging at her. Ted would be dead set against this date — if he knew. He would say that the congressman was trying to find out something about the evidence they planned to present at the upcoming hearing; or that he might simply be trying to prejudice Susan in her own work, frighten her away from their investigations. But she couldn't very well stand up Geoffrey now.

She went to the window again. The red Audi creeping along the street made up her mind. She smoothed out her jacket sleeves, picked up her handbag and drew the strap over her shoulder. In a minute, she had locked the door and was down the stairs. She had told Geoffrey to double-park, since it would be troublesome to find a parking place, and that she would meet him on the street.

'Good morning,' she said in what she hoped was an even tone as he got out on the driver's side and came around to open her door.

'Good morning yourself,' he said with a sparkle in his eyes. She was aware of her tremor of nervousness as he opened the door for her, and she slipped into the wide, low seat.

She closed her eyes as he went around to his side of the car. She knew she might as well forget her concocted reason for wanting to make this trip. For a while, she had tried to convince herself that if Geoffrey did have some ulterior motives in seeing her, she could turn the tables on him — get him to talk, make him spill his prejudices about and interest in the AHG on the issues at hand.

But as she watched him seat himself behind the wheel of the plush sports car, she knew it would be very hard indeed to play games with Geoffrey Winston.

'Let me know if you're not comfortable.

The seats are push-button adjustable,' he said.

'I see. This is fine. Plenty of leg room.'

He smiled with the obvious pride of a man who enjoyed his car. 'When you pay this much for an automobile, you ought to have a suitable place to sit. There's the cassette player. Pick what you like, unless you'd rather talk.'

She fingered a collection of tapes and picked some music to play later. But her mind wasn't really on music. The car was impressive, though. She had never been in such an expensive model.

'It's a beautiful car, and with a telephone, too,' she said, fingering the compact telephone receiver fitted snugly into the dashboard.

He smiled. 'The styling is nice, but I really bought it for the type of drive it gives. It's a good engine.' He grinned at her. 'My sons like it, too.'

'I'll bet.'

In spite of herself, her excitement mounted as they moved into traffic. Her side glance caught his relaxed expression, his neatly combed, gray-sprinkled brown hair, the pale yellow collar of his tailored shirt, his rust-colored crewneck and the gabardine trousers cut stylishly loose, though they still managed to show off his long legs and firm thighs. Excuses for having come tumbled around in Susan's mind, but she tossed them aside finally, yielding to the desire simply to enjoy herself. But she found it hard to separate Geoffrey Winston the man from Geoffrey Winston the congressman just now.

He was right about the ride. The Audi darted in and out of city traffic until they were out of Georgetown, and soon they were on the highway that would take them to colonial Williamsburg. Under Geoffrey's expert handling, the car glided along, the sensation of flight building in Susan as Washington began to drop farther and farther behind them. The car begged to move out, and with no one in front of them, Geoffrey opened up speed, but she was glad to see he was a careful driver.

'The police are notorious for pulling people over along here,' he commented about a half hour out of the city. 'So I'll keep to the speed limit.'

'That's fine with me.' Still, she could feel the untapped power of the little sports car, and the Audi hugged the curves like the ball in a roulette wheel.

As they left Washington behind, Susan breathed deeper, and glancing at Geoffrey, she thought she could see the muscles at his temples and around his mouth relax.

'Does the congressman usually get Sundays off?' she asked.

He responded with a slow smile. 'I try to. Oh, there are sometimes functions I have to attend, but I like to get out of the city.'

She laughed. 'Like high tea and kissing babies?'

'Something like that.' He kept his eyes on the road, but the smile on his lips and in his eyes told Susan he was enjoying himself. She liked being alone with him. Then she looked out her side window. If only she knew a little more about his interest in her. Dared she hope he just liked her and wanted to get to know her?

Careful, she warned herself. *He may want something. You'd better be on your guard until you find out.* Surely if Geoffrey had a specific reason for bringing her along today, he would make it known soon enough. But the companionable silence was nearly unbroken for the next hour except for comments now and then about the passing scenery. Susan found it so easy not to think, just to float along with the motion of the car skimming the highway, watching the green that was trying to announce spring in spite of the windy weather they'd been having.

As they approached Williamsburg, Susan

found herself looking forward to wandering around the little colonial town even more than she thought she would. 'I haven't been here since I was twelve,' she volunteered. 'I get so intent on work, I forget there's so much in this area to enjoy.'

'A fault many of us share. I make it a point to go on outings like this, especially when the boys are home.'

The boys. She still hadn't gotten over the fact that he had two grown-up sons. 'What sort of things do you do with them?'

'Sailing, for one thing.'

'Oh, I love sailing.'

'Perhaps you . . . ' But he let it drift off. At the same time, she was thinking her enthusiasm might have been too revealing. Then she realized that something had made him pause in what sounded like an invitation. What had made him reconsider?

But he picked up the thought. 'Perhaps you will join us sometime.'

'Yes, I'd like that.' But the joy was gone. Some intruding thought had infringed on Geoffrey's spontaneity. Susan felt a twinge of frustration and turned to stare at the trees, caught by a breeze that rocked their branches. She had accepted today's invitation on a gamble. There was the possibility nothing would come of it. But already she could feel herself rushing forward, in this somewhat mysterious relationship, into a world of outings with Congressman Geoffrey Winston. But that wouldn't do. It didn't fit — not yet. She would have to keep her imagination in the present.

Geoffrey seemed not to notice Susan's dampened spirits, and whatever thought had struck him seemed to have flown by the time they neared Williamsburg. A number of the houses and businesses in the charming colonial town had been restored and opened to tourists, but there were private homes and commercial stores, as well.

'I was twelve when my parents first brought me here on a summer vacation,' said Susan. 'That was my first real taste — the Capitol, the Smithsonian . . . ' She smiled at the memory. The heartbeat of Washington had gotten to her even then, as though she belonged there; and so she had returned.

'And you came down to Williamsburg?'

'Yes. It was exciting. I had just studied the American Revolution in school.'

His eyes lit up as he visualized her youthful enthusiasm. 'A great many debates were held here that paved the way to the Continental Congress.'

'I remember.'

They followed signs to the parking area,

which was crowded on Sunday, then waited for a shuttle bus that took them to the visitors' center, where Geoffrey paid their entrance fees and they had photos taken for their passes. Then they waited outside while the photos were developed and laminated to the clip-on passes. Geoffrey stood with his shoulder protectively angled against her, creating a feeling of intimacy. Her gaze was drawn back again to his strong jaw, firm mouth and alert eyes. Then she looked away.

She knew she shouldn't like standing so near him, shouldn't enjoy the way she could stretch herself up tall and still feel dwarfed by his height. She fought the heady sensations, but it was a losing battle with indulgence. She wanted to feel his name roll off her tongue, his title, too. *Silly*, she said. She mustn't fantasize like that. It led to other fantasies, more personal and fraught with danger.

'Susan.'

She jerked her mind back from its wandering. 'Yes.'

He lowered his head just an inch, his hand coming up to her back as if it belonged there. 'The badges are ready.'

The badges were brought to the table under an awning, and several people reached for theirs. Susan groaned at her picture, then watched Geoffrey clip his on. Even in the hastily shot photo, she could see that Geoffrey had turned on his winning smile in time for the camera. For no logical reason, a stab of pain assailed her. She must not forget that he was a politician and could turn on charm at will. She smiled perfunctorily as he fastened her badge on her jacket. Then they walked to the shuttle bus that would take them to the center of Williamsburg.

They took their seats on the bus, and Geoffrey unfolded the map made for tourists. She peered over his shoulder, catching his pine-scented after-shave as she moved to get a better view. The scent made her want to touch his sleeve, but she held back.

'What would you like to see?' he asked. The historic area was laid out along Duke of Gloucester Street, which crossed the Palace Green, at the end of which was the Royal Governor's Palace.

'Let's start at the courthouse,' she suggested. 'We can work our way down to the silversmith.'

'Good idea,' he said. 'And when we get hungry, we'll stop at the Kings' Arms Tavern.'

They spent an hour or so going through the historic district, talking with local residents in costume and examining the tools and supplies the colonials had used in their everyday life. Susan relished the feel of the rough-hewn wood and natural fibers used to make their furnishings. She especially enjoyed the wigs and curls created by the wig maker.

She didn't realize how hungry she was until Geoffrey steered her in the direction of the King's Arms Tavern. Then they stepped into the genteel atmosphere and followed the hostess to a table.

'I want everything on the menu,' she said, laughing, realizing how easy it was to laugh with Geoffrey, how much she was enjoying the day.

'That's quite a range,' he said. 'Do you want to start with the peanut soup?'

'Well, maybe not everything,' she quipped, 'but Virginia ham sounds good. Breakfast seems like a year ago.'

Geoffrey settled on roast prime rib of beef, then gave the waiter both their orders. As their eyes adjusted to the dimly lit room, Susan focused on Geoffrey's face. He took a deep breath, then slowly expelled it. He reached across the table to take her hands in his. Then he said, 'Susan, I know you don't want to talk about this, but I've been thinking a lot about your work with the AHG.'

She batted her eyelashes twice, pulling in her random thoughts suddenly. She had almost been able to forget that they might have to discuss this. 'I hadn't been thinking about that,' she said, caught off guard.

'I know,' he said, creasing his brows ever so slightly. 'But I have.'

Susan's heart thudded. Her hopes for a carefree day were dashed as Geoffrey's voice and look took on the quality of a man used to authority. She looked down at her hands in his. The disappointment stung her, and she turned her head away, withdrawing her hands.

'Susan, please. Hear me out. You know I care about what happens to you.'

Her eyes flashed as she looked up at him and said, 'How do I know that? You barely know me at all. Why would you care, anyway? Is it me or is it the AHG you care about?'

His look held a mixture of compassion and reservation, as if he wasn't sure how much he wanted to say. At that moment the waiter brought their drinks, placed them on the table and silently left again.

'If you want information from me, then ask,' she said. 'Let's stop beating around the bush. Let's get to the point.'

His face flushed, and his eyes took on a darker quality. The muscles at the ridges of his cheekbones were working, but he waited until she finished. Then he said, very deliberately, 'You really don't trust me, do you, Susan?'

'Trust you? That's not fair. I barely know you.'

'But we haven't time . . . ' He paused. His voice became low, determined. 'I want to get to know you, Susan, if you'll give me a chance.'

She jerked her chin up, but his eyes made her hold her tongue. There was something he wanted to say but couldn't. She was sure of it.

'I'm sorry. I was a bit hasty. But — ' she paused, then went on more slowly, trying to give her rioting senses and confused thoughts a semblance of order ' — you see, I appreciate your interest in us, but there's nothing you can do. We operate in confidence until we are ready to put our facts before the congressional sub-committee on which you sit.'

Susan averted her gaze, not wanting to look at him as she said, 'Ted warned me that you might be trying to pry something out of me. If that's true, I wish you'd do it now and get it over with.'

'Branagan.' The name came from between tightened jaws, and when she looked up, she was startled to see the look of intensity on Geoffrey's face. He leaned toward her, relaxing his jaw but with the intense look still in his eyes.

'I'd like to know about Ted,' he said. 'How long have you known him?'

The question was completely unexpected. She might not have been surprised had Geoffrey wanted to know something about the type of people who were coming to the AHG or about the type of false reports they suspected were being circulated about them, but she never expected Geoffrey's interest to be in Ted.

'I don't . . . I don't know what you mean.'

Geoffrey took a sip of the dark beer he had ordered, then hesitated, as if deciding how much to say. 'I wondered how closely you work with Ted Branagan.'

'Well, very closely. I don't think there's much we don't share — about work, I mean.' She frowned, hating to have to explain it this way.

'I see.'

She stared at him, but his dark brows were knitted as he studied his beer stein.

'Well, I'm afraid I don't see,' she said. 'What is it you wish to know about Ted Branagan?'

'I — ' he said, then raised his eyes to hers again. He made a move as if he wanted to reach for her hands, only she kept them safely in her lap this time. 'I know it sounds presumptuous of me, Susan, but I want you to be careful. Will you do that?'

'Careful of what? Of Ted? That's ridiculous.'

Her expression must have registered her shock, but he continued in a low, calm voice. 'I know I'm probably overreacting, but when I met you, it's just that I felt — ' he searched for words ' — responsible.'

'Responsible?' She was still struck by the incredulity of his remarks, and then, as she was still trying to make sense of what he was saying, she saw the range of emotions in his eyes.

She stifled an exclamation. Could Geoffrey be jealous of Ted? The thought was flattering but a little unreasonable, even if the idea might bring her some relief. If that was all, there was less to worry about. Perhaps Geoffrey's warnings stemmed from simple jealousy.

They both looked up as the waiter placed platters of steaming food before them, and for a moment their eyes met across the table.

'I'm sorry if I upset you, Susan. It's just that I've a lot of battle scars and I don't want you to get any.' Geoffrey's comment did not come off quite as nonchalantly as he would have liked.

She studied him, unsure how to answer.

'You're too pretty, you know,' he said, and

she could see the attempt at humor in his eyes.

'Too pretty for what?'

He flipped the linen napkin open on his lap. 'To get caught between opposing forces.'

She had been about to take a bite of ham, but she lowered her fork. 'Geoffrey Winston, I really don't understand you. What opposing forces?'

The twinkle left his eye as he looked at her intently again. 'Oh, come now, Susan. Surely you realize that for all your desire to root out corruption and reform government agencies, there are those who would prefer that they didn't get reformed. I'm not sure you're really qualified to deal with them.'

Susan groaned. 'But we've had this argument before. Those are the people we're fighting. Men in positions of power or behind the scenes who want things to stay the way they are for their own selfish reasons.'

'It's not quite the same argument. If rooting around after false reports were that easy, I wouldn't worry about you. It's just that I don't trust the people you have to come in contact with. How can you make sure of their motives?'

'What people? Whose motives?'

'Susan, have you ever stopped to think that specific people don't want you meddling in these problems and that they will go to great lengths to see that you don't succeed?'

She cocked her head. 'I suppose you're right. But we're prepared for a certain amount of roadblocks.'

He drummed his fingers on the table. 'I know you'll say it's none of my business, but I really wouldn't want to see you hurt.'

She swallowed and looked down. The growing warmth she felt when he looked at her and the desire she thought she saw in his eyes were beginning to affect her thinking processes. His words bothered her, but she couldn't get over her personal response to him. If only she could dissociate business from pleasure, just once. But it seemed that was not to be the case here.

'You said that before. Who do you think might hurt me?'

Geoffrey assessed her. His oblique warnings had not been enough. He decided to be blunt. 'Ted Branagan might hurt you, Susan. I don't trust him.'

Her eyes widened as she met his gaze. He had to be kidding. With pure shock in her voice, she asked, 'Why? What reason do you have to say that?'

'Because of allegations I've heard about Ted's background. I'm doing my best to have them investigated. I didn't want to say anything without any proof. That's not the way I operate. In fact, I didn't mean to say anything. I was curious about the AHG when I learned you were going to present evidence on false reports at a hearing. That's why I attended your press conference. It's just that I — ' he paused, his eyes brimming with emotion ' — I didn't expect to become personally involved.'

Her heart pounded in her chest as the warm sensation that had been engulfing her sent another wave along her nerves, and her body tingled in sharp response. She stared at him, unable to believe the statements he was throwing at her. Her voice was strained, almost a whisper. 'And have you . . . become personally involved?' She looked down, suddenly embarrassed.

'I have.' His voice transcended the short distance between them, and she raised her hand to clasp his, aware of the table as a barrier between them now. She felt tears — of relief, of frustration, she didn't know which. But she still hadn't resolved her dilemma.

'But what about Ted?' she asked.

'I can't really say until I find out more about him. I've been told that he was involved in some questionable activities when he was younger. If he was, then I want to know what he's doing at the AHG.'

She found this hard to believe, but even so, she asked, 'What did he do?'

Geoffrey shook his head. 'I've said enough for now — without any facts to back me up. All I can say is I have reason to believe Ted Branagan has a past, and evidently you don't know about it. If I'm right, it could affect you.'

'But how? All I do is research.'

'You find evidence that goes before House and Senate subcommittees, and you and Ted help sway the opinions of men like me to support or hinder various causes and institutions. Ted may be under the influence of men with contrary purposes to your own.'

'Oh, Geoffrey, I find this hard to believe. Ted under the influence of corrupt government officials himself?' It was so ironic she should have laughed, except that she didn't feel very amused. She thought of Ted's drive and dedication. 'He's so full of the work. I'm sure of his motives. I'm sure of him.' She frowned, trying to express her feelings. 'He does have a temper, but he's got courage. Oh, I probably can't explain it.'

Geoffrey reached to brush his thumb across her cheek, his eyes full of tenderness and warmth as he said, 'I think I understand. Has he captured your heart, as well?'

She blushed. 'No, it's not like that. He's a

good friend, that's all.'

He smiled, melancholy lingering in his eyes. 'I hope you're right, Susan, on both counts.' Then he turned his attention to his meal.

After lunch they strolled along the quiet streets and toured some of the houses. Susan felt a strong kinship with the colonials who had occupied the thriving little town in the days when the citizens were daring enough to challenge British authority. The homespun dresses worn by some of the tour guides were a symbol that the women would not wear dresses made of cloth imported from England. Rather, with their own hands, they made the cloth that covered their families.

Susan gazed at a polished round table with white clay pipes and glasses for spirits, as if the men had just gotten up and left them there. How many late-night gatherings must have taken place here with patriots plotting to overthrow England's yoke? And now she was trying to overthrow a yoke of another kind. A yoke of tyranny but one more subtle than the king's men the patriots had fought with cannons. *Our tyranny,* she thought with a shudder, *has infiltrated government agencies and is controlling them from within — some of them, anyway.* The thought depressed her. *But,* she thought, looking in a glass case at a pamphlet by Tom Paine, *we still have the right to speak out*. The AHG had been founded because they believed that people should speak out against abuse.

She looked up as Geoffrey came to look over her shoulder at the parchments and bound books on display under the glass.

'Are you ready?' he asked.

'Oh.' She moistened her lips thoughtfully. 'Yes, I suppose.'

She had felt so suddenly lost. Could the AHG really do what it had set out to do — blow the whistle on government corruption? They had succeeded in a few cases, but there was still so much to do.

Susan remembered their own late-night meetings when she had first joined. Amid Styrofoam coffee cups, ashtrays and sandwich wrappings, many a night, she, Ted, Tammy, Michael and others had sat up late reviewing their purposes and aligning their goals. They wanted to change things. They wanted to make a better world. But Geoffrey's words were beginning to depress her.

She had never before lost faith in her purpose, but his oblique warnings that all things might not be as they seemed, troubled her. And yet she didn't have the energy to fight with Geoffrey anymore. He seemed sincere. It was hard to doubt him, but he wasn't sure of his facts, either, evidently. Perhaps he was just blind to government corruption but not directly influenced by it.

Geoffrey took her hand, and they walked to the bus that would take them back to the visitors' center and parking lot. They took seats halfway back; then he very firmly took her hand in his and held it in his lap. She glanced at him quickly and saw that he had a pensive look on his face. But whatever he was thinking, he wasn't going to speak of it anymore. By the time they got to the car, she was tired from all the walking and gratefully sank into the plush seat, her head resting on the back. Geoffrey tilted the seat so she could relax completely. The dusk was comforting, and she closed her eyes.

Images from the day drifted slowly through her mind — Geoffrey opening the door for her, tickling her nose with a quill pen in one of the shops, leaning over in deep concentration to see the small pieces of metal type at the printing establishment.

By the time she raised her head, they were near Washington. As the Audi rounded a curve, she saw familiar signs. 'Have I been asleep all this time?'

He grinned. 'You must have been tired.'

'I'm sorry. It must have been a boring drive

for you.' She rubbed her eyes with her fingertips.

He glanced at her for a moment before turning his eyes back to the road. She saw the warmth and comfort in his look. 'I kind of liked it,' he said softly.

Susan shifted in her seat. Neither of them spoke. Outside the darkened car, the glimmer of apartment buildings and neon signs lined the highway. Headlights and taillights were all the evidence of civilization they had, so unbroken was the spell inside the rushing car.

'I know,' she said softly, answering some unspoken communication that had passed between them. The moment was perfect. Hadn't this been what she had subconsciously missed in life — always keeping herself so busy and throwing herself into causes so that she wouldn't know what she was missing?

How long had it been since she had shared such quiet intimacy with someone? Was it the same with Geoffrey, she wondered, studying the side of his face. 'Do you ever get lonely?' she asked suddenly, surprised at her own frankness.

'Yes,' he said. 'Oh, I have the boys a couple of times a year, and my schedule keeps me busy, but . . . yes, I get lonely.' He reached over and squeezed her hand. At that moment, she never wanted to leave him. For whatever reason he wanted her to be more careful in her work, she knew that it came from sincere motivation.

They crossed the Potomac and entered the city, the night traffic exhilarating as they drove toward Georgetown. Miraculously, there was a parking place on her street, and Geoffrey slipped the Audi into it. He turned off the motor, and they sat in silence.

'Would you like to come in?' Susan asked.

His right arm went around her shoulders, and his hand smoothed the back of her head. Then he brushed his lips across hers. 'If you'd like me to,' he said.

A slow trembling began within her. 'I'd like to show you my place,' she said.

He smiled in the dark, the reflection from the streetlights in his eyes. 'That would be nice.'

Their footsteps echoed on the brick as they crossed the street. She felt momentarily embarrassed as she fumbled for her keys.

Geoffrey followed her as she led the way upstairs. Inside the apartment, she turned on the goose-neck lamp and then automatically headed for the one over her desk. Then she paused. 'Is one lamp enough?' she asked.

'This is just fine.' The surroundings brought a smile to Geoffrey's lips. The well-used furniture, shelves full of books, the dual-purpose work-and-eating table and what looked like a tiny kitchen off the living room reminded him of his days in law school.

'Would you like something to drink?' Susan asked.

'If you're having something.'

'Well, there's tea and . . . ' She walked into the kitchen and opened the refrigerator. They hadn't had anything to eat since lunch. 'I could rustle up something to eat,' she suggested, not wanting this day of fantasy to end.

She turned, to find him looking at her with concern and longing, and she let the refrigerator door close behind her. 'Oh, Geoffrey,' she said as he came to her.

Then she was in his arms. His mouth found hers, and she relaxed against him. Away from prying eyes, she could let him hold her; she could relish his male scent and his woody cologne. Even the texture of his sweater tantalized her fingers. He exhaled a deep sigh and pulled her against him, nuzzling her hair and her ear.

There was no turning back. Not when they felt like this about each other. His lips were on her neck, and she arched her body against him, letting her arms roam around his waist. 'Geoffrey,' she whispered as his thumbs brushed across her breasts. Heat seared through her as his hands tugged at her shirt and he kissed her face. Then he bent to trace a line of kisses from her throat to her collarbone. He uttered a deep groan and held her tight, his need obvious. He smoothed her hair with his hand and whispered, 'Susan, I want to make love to you.'

She swallowed as he stepped away from her so he could look into her eyes. A pang of fear shot through her heart as she realized she still longed to cling to him. Was he going to explain it wasn't a good idea, that they must quell their passion?

Then he shook his head as if speaking to himself. 'I don't deserve you, Susan. You're too young for me.'

'Is that all you're concerned about?' she said with relief. 'My age?'

'No, that's not what I mean. I mean I don't want you to think I'm taking advantage of you. God knows, I want you. But I don't want you to do anything you'll regret.'

Regret. Somehow the word penetrated her befuddled mind. Yes. Passion, regret. Flip sides of the same coin often enough. Damn this man . . . to act as if he cared, to make her trust him and then keep her at arm's distance.

'Thank you,' she said with a cold look.

'You've reminded me that we are perhaps adversaries. I had forgotten. I had begun to believe I was someone special to you. But I see that I'm not. I merely arouse your passion. Damn you,' she choked out as the tears threatened, and she pressed her fists to his chest as he drew her near again. Then she cursed herself as she sobbed in frustration. She hadn't meant to behave this way.

'Susan, Susan, you don't understand.' He held her to him until her fists unclenched and her body sagged against him. If she had looked up, she would have seen the anguish in his face, the pain in his eyes.

He kissed her hair, her forehead and then her mouth, gently, softly, waiting for the tears to disappear. She answered his kisses, her tears tangy as they ran into her mouth and his.

Damn, he thought silently when she moved against him. She had come along and filled a void he didn't know he needed to fill. She was too precious to let go of now — too precious to get mixed up in any funny business. Damn it, how would he get her out of this?

But his thoughts were being overcome by the scent of shampoo in her hair and her faint cologne. His hands were on her again, and she responded with little moans.

Thoughts flew from her mind, as well, as

they stood entwined in each other's arms, their need building, their desire heightening. Suddenly, she smiled through the fog that had surrounded her and said, 'Perhaps we should sit down.'

'Or lie down,' he whispered, moving with her to the living room.

He took her in his embrace again. His breathing quickened, and Susan suddenly realized how much she wanted this man. The desire that had sprung from the center of her body now flooded the rest of her as she began to explore the shape of him, the clothing between them beginning to feel restricting.

As confusions of the past few days were left behind, she knew at last that this passion was meant to be satisfied, and she led him through the bedroom door.

★ ★ ★

The next morning, Susan reached over to turn off the alarm. She groaned and fell back into the bed, pulling the covers under her chin. Then, as her mind came alert, she turned her head on the pillow and looked at the rumpled blanket beside her.

A smile crept over her features, and warmth flooded her. She turned to the pillow next to her, and was greeted by a faint woody scent. Instinctively, her hand moved to her heart as she closed her eyes, envisioning Geoffrey's caress. She could still feel the tenderness of her breasts, where he'd —

But she threw the covers aside and swung her legs over the side of the bed, forcing herself to get up.

A half hour later, clothed and fed, she was at her worktable, staring at some papers that had slipped halfway out of a folder. They hadn't been that way last night. She and Geoffrey had stacked the papers on the left side of the table so they could eat on the other end.

But now her clipping file of the subcommittee members had slipped off the stack, and the papers were sticking out, lopsided. She never left anything like that. She always straightened papers in a file. She was obsessive about it.

Geoffrey had helped her stack the files. He must have seen this one. And then, later, he must have gotten out of bed. She put a hand to her cheek and sat down suddenly. Pain spread through her.

It was her own fault, but she had harbored a false hope. She shook her head, gathered her things for work and hoped unreasonably that there was some explanation.

5

Globenet, an international network of police forces, was a clearinghouse for information between police all over the world. Though a private organization with voluntary international membership, Globenet had access to government information through the Treasury Enforcement Communications System.

Susan tapped the end of her pencil on her desk blotter and gazed at the poster of Uncle Sam on the gray wall opposite. She stretched, looked at her fingernails, then tried to concentrate on her work again.

Police in one country or one state could issue all points bulletins and Wanted circulars and generally request information about suspected criminals, and any request would be circulated via computer to police all over the world. The setting up of a bureau for the purpose of rapid national and international exchange of information on criminals was not a bad idea — but it could be misused.

Susan had just confirmed that Globenet's information was on computer. Member countries filed requests either to the headquarters in France or to branch offices such as the one in Washington, located in the Treasury Building. But Globenet was an independent organization, answerable to no government. Why was it in the Treasury Building, she wondered. What bothered her was that there didn't seem to be an adequate system to control what information got into the computer bank or who used it. And from the interviews they'd conducted, they had evidence that even after the real criminal was found and convicted, suspects' names were not removed from the files.

The door flew open, and Ted burst into the room, strode across to Susan's desk, and slapped down a sheaf of papers in front of her. 'What do you think of this?' he said.

'What?'

'Globenet's got access to all the intelligence agencies in the United States through their computer hookup with the Treasury Enforcement Communication System.'

'I've been reading something about that, but which ones?'

'The FBI's National Crime Information Center, the U.S. Customs Service, the IRS Intelligence Division and the IRS Inspection Service, among others. It must be the biggest source of personal data in the Western world, and the data are interchangeable among member countries.'

'Seems like a big hole in national security. Who decides what information can be released from the intelligence agencies into Globenet's computer?'

He gave her a smug look. 'That is what we're going to find out.'

She fanned the pile of papers she had been reading so that they slapped the surface of her desk like a deck of cards. 'Well, why aren't there some sort of government controls on this?'

Ted strode over to his desk, scraped the chair back and flung himself down. 'Perhaps someone with a vested interest doesn't want there to be,' he suggested.

'And how does this have a bearing on false reports?'

'I'm not sure yet, but I have a feeling Globenet is very much involved in the circulation of false reports. After all, it is *the* clearinghouse for the criminal information circulated all over the world.'

'Hmm. I begin to see what you mean.'

He leaned forward. 'You know something else I don't like? Globenet originated in France just before the war. Their headquarters are still located in Paris. The secretary-general, Louis LeBlanc, is a Frenchman. Don't forget that according to French law, a suspect is guilty until proved innocent — the opposite of our own system.'

'So if Globenet gets your identity mixed up with that of a criminal, you're not necessarily who you say you are unless you can prove it.'

'That's right.' He shook his head.

'You really believe Globenet is at the root of our present problem? That they're the ones harassing these people who complain of false reports?'

'Yes. We don't have the proof, of course. But I think it would pay to dig into the organization. Why don't you look up its history.'

'All right.'

'We have to find out why . . . ' He shrugged.

She frowned in concentration, following Ted's thought. 'Why they would condone or encourage the circulation of false reports.'

'Yeah.'

She made a few notes, then glanced at Ted out of the corner of her eye. She felt a little guilty not telling him about Geoffrey. She rationalized that she owed him no explanation. Her personal life was none of his business, was it? But stealing a glance at him, she felt a sinking feeling for holding something back from him. She'd never had to lie to Ted in the past.

She drew lines on the paper in front of her,

guilt turning to remorse. What had Geoffrey seen in that file that lay with its contents strewn on the table? Nothing confidential was in it, she was sure. That file had contained research on the subcommittee members, nothing Geoffrey couldn't find for himself in newspapers or in the *Congressional Record*.

But there was more to it than that. It was the feeling of betrayal. He had been sneaking about in her living room after he had made love to her.

A pool of tears gathered in the corners of her eyes, the hurt forming a knot in her chest. She put her hand to her forehead and kept her face toward the papers on her desk, hoping that to anyone observing her she would look as if she were studying whatever was before her.

Her thoughts ran on, recriminations piling one on top of the other. She tried to remember what she'd said at dinner with Geoffrey. She hadn't given anything away, had she? She had thought that was the crux of the matter. If she kept confidential information to herself, what was the harm in seeing him? And there might be something to be gained — at least she had justified it that way to herself. If he were in some way associated with Globenet himself, and she could find out . . .

She dabbed the tears with her fingertips, her grief subsiding a bit, and rational thought beginning to return. She would see Geoffrey again — confront him. She would just ask him outright what he'd been doing with her files that night. Perhaps he'd have an answer. If not, then she would know what to do.

Susan spent the rest of the day buried in work, trying to keep her personal problems at bay. At five-thirty, after everyone else had left, she and Ted went through the motions of stacking papers and locking up confidential reports in file drawers. Then Ted asked, 'Want to work tonight?'

She paused. She hadn't planned on it. But what excuse could she give? Then she shrugged. 'All right. Want to come to my place?'

'Sure. It's probably cleaner than mine.'

She laughed. 'Since when has that been a prerequisite?'

He looked at her as if he didn't find that funny. 'I'll pick up some food on the way over.'

They gave a last check around the office, then locked up. Now that they were getting in deeper with the false-reports cases, they were being even more careful about leaving information lying around. Important papers were kept in the safe in the bathroom. Not that most people would make heads or tails out of the data, but they now had on hand copies of some of the documents their clients had succeeded in getting released from law-enforcement agencies by using the Freedom of Information Act. If the wrong person got hold of them, it might complicate matters. Locking everything up was just a good precaution, especially since the break-in.

As they walked toward the elevator, Susan asked, 'Do you think anyone would want to, uh, sabotage us?'

'Why do you ask?'

'Oh, it's just that I got to thinking. We're getting into some hot topics. There might be people who want to stop us before we blow the whistle on them.'

The elevator came. 'Of course,' he said as they stepped in. 'But don't tell me you've just now thought of that.'

'No, of course not. It's just that I've been concentrating on the people we help, not the — '

'Danger?'

She nodded, feeling foolish. They walked out to the street and broke their stride for some pedestrians to pass. As they walked to their cars, Susan shivered, even though it wasn't very cold out. Then she tried to shake off her mood. All jobs came with a certain amount of responsibility. 'I'm sorry, Ted. I'm just being morose.'

Ted eyed her curiously as she unlocked her car door. 'If there's something on your mind, you can tell me about it, Susan. Has someone said something?'

How could she put this into words without bringing down an avalanche? 'I told you about Congressman Winston?' She could feel Ted's instant reaction, but he waited for her to say more. 'What he suggested, well . . . it's beginning to bother me a little.' She wished she could explain to Ted. It would help so much.

But Ted's brows came down in a dark mass of accusation. His mouth went into a rigid line, and he squared his shoulders. 'Susan, I'm concerned about this congressman. I don't like it. I think we'd better go over it again.'

She lowered her gaze. 'If you want to.' She turned to her car. 'I'll tell you about it at my place. Give me an hour to freshen up, okay?' As she settled herself in the car a sense of anger came over her. Well, she thought, jamming her key into the ignition, she would just have to tell Ted, even though he wasn't going to be sympathetic.

She tossed Ted a nod as she backed out of

her parking place and headed for the street. A bubble had burst. Tears of anger threatened to spill.

There was a secret world two people shared when they were discovering their love, and in spite of her doubts about Geoffrey, Susan could feel herself falling in love with him. At least she wanted the chance to speak to him again, to confront him on the matter of the rifled papers, find out for herself if he really had gone through them behind her back.

But Ted's challenging her made her feel cheated. She needed to sort this relationship out for herself. It wasn't time to talk about her feelings to anyone else. And now she had to let Ted into what ought to be a closed circle. It wasn't fair.

'Oh, come on,' she said aloud as she drove through traffic. She was a grown woman. If this little bubble had burst, surely she could deal with it.

She parked in the garage and went around the house. Once inside her apartment, she straightened up the living room and work area, then went to wash her face and hands.

In half an hour the buzzer rang. She buzzed the downstairs door open and heard heavy footsteps coming up the carpeted stairs in the hall.

'Just a minute,' she called from the

bedroom, then walked in her stocking feet to open the door.

Geoffrey stood there, a bottle of wine in one hand. He leaned against the door frame, smiling. He was about to kiss her, but the shocked look on her face stopped him dead.

'What?' She gasped, but her mouth didn't form the rest of the question. Embarrassment flooded her, and for a moment they just stared at each other.

Then slowly, with deliberation, he lowered his arm and straightened his stance. 'I'm sorry. I didn't mean to surprise you. I should have called. But I was shopping for my son's birthday present, and I passed by . . . ' For a moment neither spoke.

Then Susan managed to say, 'Come in, Geoffrey. I didn't mean to react that way. It's just that I was, uh, expecting someone else.'

Her heart still raced as she smiled apologetically. 'It's a business meeting . . . Ted is . . . ' She searched for the right words, for she knew how Geoffrey felt about Ted. She had not told him that she and Ted often worked at her apartment.

Geoffrey stood stiffly, the affection flown from his face. He strode into the room and set the wine bottle down on the table. Then he turned to face her.

'I'm sorry. I didn't realize I'd be interrupting anything.' He started for the door.

'Wait a minute. You've no reason to be angry. We work here — to go over plans away from the phones at the office. It's not what you think . . . ' She didn't know how to finish. She felt irritated having to explain that she and Ted were not lovers.

Geoffrey's eyes were veiled. 'It's all right. I should have thought you might have company. I'll go. Honestly, it's all right.' He turned away, miffed, and Susan's heart lurched. She swallowed hard, trying to form the words for what she had to say next. 'Geoffrey,' she said, stopping his retreat to the door.

He turned, the barrier still drawn up between them.

She cleared her throat and looked him in the eye. 'This,' she said, picking up the folder of clippings off her worktable. 'Do you know what's in it?'

He frowned, the lines about his eyes and mouth harsh now, his defenses down. 'How could I?' he said, looking from the folder to her.

'Geoffrey,' she said sighing, 'please tell me the truth. I found it on my table the night we . . . ' Her voice started to break, and she had to clear her throat again. Then she continued. 'I had left it on the pile, but in the morning . . . '

Suddenly he seemed to comprehend what she was asking, and he squared his shoulders, his dark eyes penetrating. 'Susan, if you want to know if I've been looking through your papers, you are mistaken. My sleeve brushed that stack, knocking it over, as I passed the table on my way to the kitchen. I tried to replace the pile, but if I got things out of order, I'm sorry. A few things did fall out.' He shook his head. 'I saw my picture. You really are thorough.'

She stared at him, trying to determine whether he was telling the truth. She wanted desperately to believe him. But was that all there was to it — sloppiness in restacking the files so that they had fallen again later, curiosity over seeing his own photo?

By now Geoffrey was glancing around the room as if inspecting it for safety. 'You'll be all right?'

'Well, of course. Why shouldn't I be?' Then she remembered that Geoffrey didn't trust Ted. 'Oh, don't be silly. We've worked here a hundred times. I told you, there's nothing to worry about.'

He frowned. 'I know. I'm just being protective.' Then he pulled her to him for a kiss. It was rough, possessive.

She broke away and said, 'Really, Geoffrey. I've got to work tonight.' And in a more somber tone, she added, 'I'm sorry — if I'd known you were coming, I could have — '

'I know. Too bad.' He brushed some lint off his jacket and cleared his throat. 'All right. Another time.'

She attempted a smile and led him to the door, knowing she still needed time to evaluate what he'd told her. As he turned at the threshold to say goodbye, she said, 'Oh, by the way, I'm going to tell Ted about . . . us tonight. I think it will clear the air.'

But instead of the congratulatory smile she expected, a shadow passed over his eyes. 'Do you think that's wise?'

'Of course, Geoffrey. Don't you see? Ted and I have worked very closely for a long time. I'm not used to keeping things from him, and besides, maybe he should know I'm seeing you. I just thought it would clear the air all the way around.'

'I thought you said it was a business relationship.'

'It is, but we're friends, too. I just don't like to lie.'

'I'm not asking you to lie.'

'But it's like a lie, not to tell him we — '

Geoffrey shook his head. 'It's not a lie. You don't have to tell people about what is just between us. I just think it would be better if you didn't mention it quite yet.' His eyes had that hurt look, as if he wanted to say more but couldn't, and she felt herself wanting to melt into his arms again.

'If you don't leave pretty soon, you won't have a choice,' she said, turning her face away in an attempt to escape his eyes and the effect his gaze had on her temperature. 'Ted will be here in five minutes, and he's usually on time.'

But he seemed reluctant to go. 'Susan, please understand. I just want to satisfy myself about Ted's background.'

She bit back the words 'And he wants to be sure of yours.' But she did say, 'Sounds like something we would do. Part of my job is digging up the past on people we deal with, you know.' She knew she was taunting him, and the pained look in his eyes made her want to bite her tongue. It wrenched her heart to have hurt him.

'Oh, Geoffrey, I'm sorry. I didn't mean it that way.' But it was too late. The shield went up, and he turned to go.

'It's all right. I know I deserved that.'

'But you . . .'

'We'll talk later, Susan. I'm sorry I came at a bad time.' He waved and then went on down the stairs, his shoulders hitched up in an attitude of self-preservation.

'Blast,' Susan said, pounding the doorjamb with her fist. That certainly hadn't solved anything. She shook her head and turned away when she heard the downstairs door bang shut and Ted come rushing up.

She barely had time to move out of the way before he burst into the room, his face a cloud of anger, a notebook sliding out from under one arm, the pizza box swinging dangerously on the end of a string.

Susan reached both hands to take the pizza. 'Don't say it. I know. You ran into Geoffrey Winston downstairs. Yes, he was here. You want to know what he was doing here. Sit down.' She placed the pizza on the table and pointed to the sofa.

'Susan.'

'Ha! See, you can't even let me have the last word, or the first, in this case.'

'Susan Franks, what are you up to?' He did not sit but remained standing so that he could challenge her at eye level.

She sighed. 'Nothing. I was just going to explain. I'm sorry, Ted, but I really am tired of feeling like a Ping-Pong ball.'

He started to say something, then seemed to think better of it. Instead, he paced across the rug as she tore the cover off the box and went to the kitchen for a knife and paper plates.

Unable to wait any longer, Ted finally exploded. 'Well, you said you were going to tell me!'

'I am, I am. Just let me get my bearings.' She set the knife and plates down and pulled soda cans out of a paper bag Ted had brought with the pizza.

'Ted, I was planning to tell you everything this evening. I can't stand having secrets from you. You know how much your friendship means to me.'

'Thanks,' he said, but he gave her a sour look.

She continued. 'I admit I'm attracted to Geoffrey Winston, and — ' she looked down ' — he is to me. I tried to fight it at first. I mean, I agreed with you that he might be trying to get something out of us. But after I spoke with him about it, I don't think so.'

Ted was listening, but the storm on his face hadn't abated. 'Actually, he's interested in us. He's very anxious to hear our evidence. In fact, I think he's on our side.'

'Did he say that?'

'Well, no, not really. We didn't talk about specifics. But we share — that is, we agree on many other things.'

Ted's eyes drilled into her, and he cocked his head in an attitude of mockery. She realized it was going to be harder to get out of her predicament than she had expected.

'How long has this been going on?' He sounded like an old record.

She lowered a brow in annoyance and yanked the top off her soda can. She decided to sit down even if he didn't. 'I told you. I met him a week ago Saturday at the National Archives. I saw him again last Sunday.'

'I mean, how did the relationship leap from a chance encounter to a surprise visit on a Tuesday evening? Getting awfully cozy, aren't you? Or maybe he was trying to check up on you. Ever think of that? You shouldn't let just anyone into your apartment, Susan. Especially when you've got work lying about.' The covert hostility in his tone stung her. But she was determined to hold her ground.

'He was shopping for his son, and — ' Her face reddened.

'His son?'

'Yes. He has two. Sixteen and twenty, if you want to know.'

Ted remained silent, no longer grilling her but letting the weight of the silence carry his message.

Susan took a deliberate bite of pizza. Finally, hunger overcame Ted's posturing, and he sat down opposite her and wedged a slice out of the box and onto his plate. But he chewed slowly, watching her.

'Ted, really. I don't know why you're so upset about this. Just because Geoffrey Winston happens to be on the subcommittee before which we're to appear doesn't mean he has ulterior motives in seeing me.'

'How do you know he doesn't? How do you know he's not trying to steer us away from unraveling the false reports issue because he might have something to cover up?'

'I don't. I don't.' She took another bite and tried to organize her thoughts. 'In fact, Geoffrey said that we should be careful. He said people may want to foil our plans. But I can't think how we can be any more careful. If we're going to accuse someone of being responsible for circulating false reports to harass private citizens, I guess Geoffrey thinks that the party may want to know before the hearing what we found out. I agree with you that we should prevent that from happening. But I'm convinced Geoffrey is with us, not against us, and so I can guarantee there's no danger from that quarter.'

Ted's look was still hostile. 'I've thought of all that, of course.'

She retorted in a similar tone, 'Oh, forgive me. I didn't mean to imply that the congressman had thought of anything we hadn't already.'

She didn't mean to sound so biting, but the two men's attitudes toward each other were getting on her nerves. If they could all just do their job and stop suspecting each other ... It seemed so childish to behave this way.

Then she remembered Geoffrey's allegations about Ted's past. How could she ask him about that without making it sound as if she didn't trust him?

'Ted, you haven't ever met Geoffrey, have you?'

'Of course not. I just think he has reasons for trying to keep you away from your work.'

She scrutinized him. Something about the way he answered her query left room for doubt, but she let it drop. And Geoffrey wasn't exactly trying to keep her away from her work, she thought. She studied Ted as he sat opposite her.

After getting the anger off his chest, Ted seemed more able to give serious thought to the work at hand. He made no more comments about Geoffrey Winston, and Susan hoped he was going to let the matter drop.

Finally, they came back to the matter of their own safety.

'You know where the danger would come from, don't you?' Ted said.

'Well, from the agencies or persons who

have the most to lose if we expose them, those with a vested interest.'

'Yes.' He eyed her intently. 'And the evidence seems to be leading us in one direction.'

'Globenet,' she said. Then she drummed her fingers on the table. 'But we only suspect that. We can't prove it.'

'Well, we'd never be able to prove it ourselves. All we can do is present the evidence we have of false reports and hope the subcommittee recommends that a full congressional investigation into Globenet's background and function is in order.' He glanced idly at a corner of the room. 'Hmm,' he said, 'that would be a feather in our cap — a full-scale investigation into the workings of Globenet to decide whether it violates the rights of private citizens.'

Susan leaned forward, her elbows on the table, her fingers massaging her temples. 'Globenet,' she said. 'An all-powerful organization subject to no one's scrutiny but its own, with access to the data banks of the world's intelligence and police files. It's an obvious place for anyone who wants power, to gain control.' She dropped her hands to the table. 'But what purpose is there in circulating these lousy false reports about ordinary people or petty crimes? It just seems like a huge waste of time. Their own statistics show that only a small percentage of the cases that go through their clearinghouse result in arrests, and they're mostly small fry. Why don't they go after the really big fish?'

'The obvious answer is that the police of the world are being led away from the bigger criminals.'

'But who specifically are the police being led away from? And by whom?'

'I don't know. Perhaps Globenet has a skeleton in its closet.' He frowned, picking up a pencil and thumping its eraser against the table. 'Each answer just leads to another question.'

Susan yawned. 'Ted, I'm pretty tired. Do you think we've done enough for tonight? I can't think of anything more.'

'Me neither. I just hope that the subcommittee concludes that there's something fishy within Globenet and that it merits a closer look.'

'If we do it right, how can they not? Remember our policy,' she said.

'Uh-huh. Don't present anything we haven't documented. Present the facts in the order that will lead them to the conclusion we want.'

'And when we answer questions, we stick to the facts,' she reminded him, 'and ask them to draw their own conclusions.'

'Right.' It had worked before. They held each other's gaze for a moment. Strong in purpose, strong in agreement. No wonder there was such a bond between them, Susan thought. Two people couldn't be so committed to a cause without having a strong esprit de corps.

She relaxed. She was glad she'd told Ted about Geoffrey. He might not like it, but at least he knew, and she didn't have to feel as if she were sneaking around.

But she was totally unprepared for what Ted did next. As she stood up to place the notes she'd made in a folder, he came around the table and casually took her arm. She looked up, expecting him to say something. But instead, his arms went around her waist, and he gently but firmly pulled her to him and kissed her.

She wriggled in his grasp. 'Ted,' she said after she had twisted her mouth away from his, 'what's this?'

But he captured her mouth again, and she had no choice but to remain where she was. Ted was an attractive man, but why had he waited until now to make a move? It seemed as if her finding another love interest had aroused Ted's jealousy. But she would never have planned it this way.

She only returned the kiss halfheartedly. She didn't know what he was up to, but she didn't want to start another argument.

He finally let go of her mouth and looked into her eyes.

'Ted Branagan, what was that supposed to mean?'

He cocked an eyebrow. 'Don't tell me you don't know what it means when a man kisses a beautiful woman?'

'Ha!' She leaned back in his arms, since he did not seem disposed to let her go. 'But you've never kissed me before. Not like that, anyway.'

Now he looked more serious, and she imagined for an instant that she saw real disappointment in his eyes. 'I know,' he said. 'I know, Susan. It's not that I haven't felt it. It was — ' he half turned from her ' — superstition, I guess you'd call it.'

'How do you mean?'

'Oh, you know, you don't mix business with pleasure.'

'Pleasure?' She could hardly keep the incredulity out of her voice.

He turned back to her. 'But I want you to know, Susan, that if you want a relationship, you don't have to look any further.'

'That's nice of you, Ted, but I swear I thought it was supposed to be women who

140

were hard to understand. All of a sudden, I've got two of the . . . ' She didn't finish, seeing the instant resentment in his eyes.

'Oh, I don't mean . . . ' To compare? But that was exactly what she did mean, only she couldn't say it. Suddenly, she felt sorry for him. She had no reason to step on his toes. She reached for his hands. Compassion and deep friendship welled up in her.

'You know I never want to lose you as a friend, Ted.'

'Do you think it could ever be more than that?'

Oh, the irony in that question. *Yes, yes, it could have been more than that. Last year, last month. But not now!*

'You never said anything before, Ted.'

He tried to give her a joking smile, but it didn't quite come off. 'Missed my chance, have I?'

Perhaps there really was more to Ted than she had thought. And she had thought she knew him. She had been mistaken.

'What a pitiful pair we are. I don't know what to say.'

He reached out and put his hand on her face in a tender gesture that was unlike him. She looked into his eyes and saw a range of emotions she never knew dwelt there.

'Oh, Ted, I'm sorry. I really didn't know.'

She turned abruptly, afraid she would mislead him. For while she loved Ted as a friend, she had never felt for him the passion that Geoffrey had aroused in her. But she did care for Ted, and she didn't want to hurt him.

'Ted,' she said as he got his jacket on and headed for the door, notebook in hand, 'I guess I'm not very good at saying things like this, but you do mean a lot to me.'

He paused at the door and smiled, a little sadly. 'I know, Susan. I guess I just don't want to lose you, either. I don't want to lose what we've got.'

She knew what he meant. They were a good team. If she fell in love with someone else, things wouldn't be the same. Up until now they had shared everything. They'd been immersed in their causes. Now part of her would be revealed only to someone else. Only to Geoffrey.

She smiled meekly at Ted and squeezed his arm as he went out. Then she closed the door and rested her hand on the door frame as she turned the lock.

Susan pondered again why Ted had never made an advance before. They had certainly spent a lot of time together. But perhaps he had sensed that she wasn't looking for that sort of thing. And she hadn't been. She had always been very definite about the borderline between their relationship and her independent status. For before meeting Geoffrey, she'd been happy on her own. She didn't have to answer to anyone, and she must have let Ted see that in subtle ways. She had gotten used to independence. Now it was frustrating not only to have one man questioning her moves but two.

Since the matter was resolved at least for the night, she went to the bedroom to undress and put on her terry-cloth robe. As she did so, she mulled over what she and Ted had concluded. They had heard enough cases now to be certain that someone was circulating false and incomplete reports on private citizens among the law-enforcement agencies of the United States and possibly the world. If nothing else, a suspect's name ought to be removed from the criminal-information data banks when the real criminal was found and a conviction made. A person's record shouldn't be held against him after he was proved innocent, and in at least a dozen cases these oversights had cost people their jobs, damaged their credit and infringed on their rights in many other ways.

She returned to the worktable to clear up. As she did so, she felt a prickly sensation on her back. She raised her head just in time to see a man's face peering into her window.

Panic rushed through her. The face disappeared, but she was shaking now. She leaped to turn off the lights so he couldn't see in. She double-checked the door lock.

She could call the police, but by the time they got here, he would be gone. Her heart still pounded as she edged toward the telephone. He had probably climbed the creepers that covered the house. But why?

At least she would call the landlords, the couple who lived downstairs, to warn them. She knew the Millers' number by heart.

'Hello?'

'Elizabeth, this is Susan,' she said breathlessly. 'I just saw a man at the window. He must have climbed the vines. Would you have Charles take a look?'

'A man in the window?' Elizabeth's voice, sharpened by the emergency, addressed her husband. 'Charles, Susan says there's a man in the window. Go out and see. Hurry.' Then she came back to the phone.

'All right, Susan. Don't worry. Charles will take care of it. I'll call the police. Do you want to wait down here?'

'No, thank you. I'm all right.' She put down the phone and took a few deep breaths. By now she had the courage to go to the window and look out. Nothing was there. Only the streetlight from across the street cast

144

a dim glow over the sidewalk below. A few leaves turned over on the brick street. She could see the vines at the side of the window, like fingers gripping the sides of the house.

Ten minutes later her phone rang. 'Susan? Elizabeth. Charles says no one is there now. The police are coming. Are you sure you saw somebody?'

'Yes, I'm pretty sure,' she said, though she wasn't sure she could describe the face. 'I'll talk to the police. You can send them up.' She hung up the phone and put her clothes back on to talk to the police. Then she went to the kitchen and searched below the sink for a can of Mace she kept there. She read the instructions, never having used it before. As she brought the can to the living room and looked for a suitable place to keep it, she realized her hands were shaking. So, it had come to this. Of course, the man might just be a Peeping Tom. She would have to ask the police if there had been other complaints.

Five minutes later, two burly policemen trod up the stairs and tapped on her door. She let them in and gave them the details. She couldn't describe the man very well, only that his face seemed dark — but that might have been the shadows — and his hair seemed very black and thick. The policemen

145

seemed mildly interested when she mentioned her job, but they didn't dwell on it. Finally, their notes taken, they stood up to leave.

'Thank you, Miss Franks. I'm sorry you were bothered.' The older man looked weary, as if his own job was much too hard for him. There was probably far too much crime in this city for any police force to keep up with, and his next words proved it.

'If you'd like to come down to headquarters, we have files of about four thousand photographs you could look through. Do you think you could identify the man?'

'I'll look at the photos if you think it'll help. But I only had a glimpse of him.'

'It's up to you,' he said, snapping his book shut. 'Criminals change appearances, and you yourself said it was dark.'

'It probably wouldn't help, then,' she said, depressed to think that even if she tried to identify the intruder, it was probably a very long shot and not worth the time.

'All right. We'll let you know if we catch up with him. We might ask you to look at a lineup.' But his eyes said it was doubtful they would ever catch the man, whoever he was.

She saw the policemen to the door, then turned and walked to the center of the room, eyeing the window warily. If someone was trying to scare her, she was determined to defeat him. She took one of the books that had been lying on her worktable and went to bed. She stared at the book, but her mind kept wandering to the face at the window and her conversation with the police. By the time she had turned five pages, it was four in the morning. Finally, exhaustion caught up with her, and she dropped the book on the floor and slept.

The alarm woke her at 8:00 A.M. The sun peeked through the tops of the maples, elms and sycamores that lined the narrow street outside and cast dappled shadows on the house. She pulled herself out of bed and went to look out. In the daylight, the street looked so harmless. It was the night that so often induced fear.

As the coffee percolated, she gathered her papers together. She was tired, but she felt better having something to do. She wouldn't be able to sleep, anyway, if she stayed home.

She supposed she ought to mention the prowler to Geoffrey. But thinking about Geoffrey made her feel more distant from him somehow. Even as her pulse quickened with the mention of his name, there were too many thoughts confusing her to enjoy the beginnings of a relationship with him. It might be best if they didn't see each other before the hearings began. Perhaps she should keep to herself for a while, to concentrate on work. Then when she walked into the sub-committee hearing, she would be at her best. They would win Congress over to their side; and a full-scale investigation into Globenet's activities would be launched. And prowlers be damned.

6

Susan and Ted walked briskly along the sidewalk to the Rayburn House of Representatives Office Building. The sun had come out, and it finally looked as if it was going to stay warm. The leafy green of Capitol Hill announced that spring was here to stay.

Susan felt the way a performer feels before going onstage — excited but with everything under control. Her pulse throbbed with expectation as they climbed the steps. Ted held the door open for her. His green eyes sparkled, and the color in his ruddy cheeks told her that he was just as tense and expectant as she was.

Their heels clicked on the marble floor as they walked toward the elevator that would take them to room 2255, where the subcommittee hearing was scheduled to take place. They would present their statements today on the issue of false reports circulating among law-enforcement agencies, in the hope that the subcommittee would decide to fully investigate Globenet. Since the United States paid half a million dollars a year for membership in the agency, Susan knew

Globenet would not be pleased if they knew that the AHG's ultimate goal was to curtail U.S. involvement in the operation. But first they must lead this subcommittee to the conclusions they had reached as they had sifted through evidence relating to false reports.

Outside the door to room 2255, the congressional subcommittee members chatted in groups. When Susan spotted Geoffrey standing against the dark paneled doorway talking with Ernest Smith, Republican from Utah, a surge of excitement rushed through her. She recognized Gerhardt Schilingham, Republican from Pennsylvania, and Chalmers Bingham, Democrat from New York.

As Susan and Ted approached him, Irwin Bradshaw looked up and gave them a once-over. Bradshaw had aroused in her an uncomfortable feeling ever since she had researched the members of this subcommittee. The other men seemed straightforward enough in their political bents, but Bradshaw was hard to pin down.

She tried to shake off the feeling as she nodded to the representatives she passed and walked into the room. As she passed Geoffrey, her chin went up slightly, and their eyes met.

'Hello,' she said.

'Hello.' he answered. There was warmth in his gaze, and she longed to stop and touch his arm, but she dared not. Today they were professionals. They would have to put aside the personal feelings that had developed between them — until the hearing was over.

Ted followed her into the room, and they walked to their seats at a long, polished walnut table in the center of which microphones rested. A pitcher of water and several glasses were within reach. At the front of the room was a raised dais with seats for all the congressmen. Microphones were placed between each pair of seats. An American flag stood beside the windows at the front of the room. This hearing would not be broadcast, though it was open to the public.

Susan saw Congressman Smith consult his watch and then gesture to his colleagues, who followed him in and took their seats.

'Good afternoon,' Congressman Smith said from the center of the dais. 'The Subcommittee on Law Enforcement and Information Exchange will now come to order. Today's subcommittee begins a review of the issue of false reports allegedly circulating within U.S. law-enforcement agencies.' The hearing had begun.

Smith went on to explain that they would hear a statement presented by Chairman Ted

Branagan and Research Director Susan Franks from the Association for Honesty in Government on the violation of human rights by the alleged circulation of false reports among U.S. law-enforcement agencies in this country.

'We will hear Mr. Branagan's statement first. Then we will proceed with questions concerning the evidence. We will break for lunch and resume this afternoon at two o'clock. At this time I would like to recognize Mr. Ted Branagan for his statement.'

Susan looked across the room at Geoffrey, who had taken his seat on the dais. His face was all attention, and she could feel her heart beat leap up a notch. She thought she saw him give her a slight nod, then he turned his attention to Ted, who leaned forward to read his statement into the microphone in front of him.

'Mr. Chairman and members of the subcommittee, the Association for Honesty in Government is a grassroots organization whose purpose is to aid private citizens who have been abused by misconduct in government sectors,' he began. His voice was confident, determined. 'We have made it known that those with grievances could come to us and ask for counseling on how best to raise their voice against the government when they have been wronged.

'Through a number of interviews, the summaries of which you have before you, it has become apparent that false reports concerning these private citizens have been circulated among law enforcement agencies within this country, and we feel an investigation is called for. I will cite here a few specific examples.'

He went on to quote from the documents and to paint the picture of private citizens caught in a web of red tape, altered data, mistaken identity and bureaucratic runaround with regard to their own personal dossiers. Some merely had last names, the same as criminal suspects, but had no connection whatever with the crime committed. Some were relatives of suspected criminals. Some were suspects themselves but innocent of any wrongdoing. One citizen they had talked to had been taken into custody on suspicion of burglary. He had done nothing, but he had been in the same neighborhood in which a prowler had been reported. Later, the burglar was caught, but the original suspect's record remained in the files. All of their clients were listed somewhere in police files as having a record. And it was these records that the AHG sought to clear eventually. However, Ted reminded them, the point of the hearing was to establish that such false reports existed, and to discern their source.

He didn't come right out and say that they thought Globenet was behind this in some way, but that would come in time. First, the cases.

Susan followed Ted's speech with her eyes moving down her copy of the statement, which would be made part of the record. She glanced at Ted every so often, but she could see that he had the room at his command. She observed him making eye contact with every congressman in turn, and she observed their reactions when she could catch them.

Many of the members returned only polite stares. She thought she perceived an additional alertness in Geoffrey, and she felt her face warm as she took in his taut figure. Something beneath his usual polish made her sense that he was waiting for something — that was it. But for what? For Ted to slip up? She was still aware of the tension that existed between the two, and she felt caught between them like a piece of filing between two magnets.

Bradshaw sat back in his chair, his eyes narrow slits. Was he asleep? No, he occasionally picked up the paper in front of him and opened his eyes to study it. She shifted in her seat.

Susan read aloud from the documents their clients had gotten released from law-enforcement agencies, some by using the Freedom of Information Act. As she glanced up, she saw that Geoffrey's face was still drawn tight, his expression carefully controlled. She felt that her own formally pleasant look was plastered across her face in the same manner. Her professional mask. But she couldn't allow her thoughts to stray from what she was saying.

She finished, and Ernest Smith sat forward. 'Thank you, Miss Franks. I am sure the committee has questions. I suggest a ten-minute break to stretch our legs.'

They stood. She and Ted smiled at each other. *Off to a good start*, their look said. Then she turned to look at Geoffrey, who had caught her smiling at Ted and now looked displeased. Her eyes widened, and she poured a glass of water from the pitcher in front of her to wet her cracked lips.

She swallowed and looked at Geoffrey again. He was rotating a shoulder to get the cricks out of his neck. Drat the formal surroundings. There was no chance to say anything to him. His look had been accusatory, but then he turned to answer a comment Schilingham made.

The hearing resumed, and Congressman

Smith called for questions. Ted would answer them unless he wanted to turn them over to Susan.

Schilingham said, 'Do I understand you to say that many of these Wanted circulars and criminal dossiers contain information about investigations that have not resulted in convictions?'

Ted took the question. 'That is correct.'

'And these reports are circulated among law enforcement agencies through Globenet channels?'

'Yes. The secretary general of Globenet has stated that it is impossible to keep statistics on the number of convictions resulting from cases handled through Globenet channels. But we also have the testimony of Robert Mueller, the systems analyst who set up the computer at Globenet in 1979. He explains that the filing system can be handled in minutes by a well-trained operator.'

'Thank you.'

This was one of the questions she and Ted had rehearsed. Again she felt pride in their way of working. It was their thoroughness that made the difference.

Mr. Smith asked, 'If persons suspect that a false report has been circulated about them, how can the situation be rectified?'

Ted deferred to Susan this time. 'There is

very little chance for a person suspected of committing a crime to correct false information, especially if the records are in Globenet's data bank; for Globenet is seeking immunity from the Freedom of Information Act.'

'Thank you,' said Smith.

Geoffrey raised a hand, and Chairman Smith called on him.

'Mr. Branagan.' Geoffrey's voice boomed across the room, making Susan jump. 'Are you suggesting that coordinating the police forces of the world in an effort to apprehend criminals through the use of computer data banks is a bad idea?'

In the split second of silence before Ted delivered his answer, the room seemed to rock before Susan. How totally unexpected, and the question was delivered with a subtle antagonism that she never expected from Geoffrey. She stopped breathing for a moment. What could he possibly mean?

'No, sir, I don't.' The ruddy color in Ted's cheeks and the clipped manner in which the words came forth were the only signs that Ted was equally annoyed with the question. 'But the potential for abuse exists,' he continued. 'If a system does not have adequate checks and balances, and if this massive exchange of information is above the law, then it is a bit — ' he paused for effect ' — Orwellian.'

Geoffrey nodded in response to Ted's answer, then hit them with his next question. 'And why is it that the private individuals who came to you did not first seek justice through their own local courts or legal aid societies?'

Susan stared, aghast. Did he still think they were nothing more than rabble-rousers? A knot of anger coiled in the pit of her stomach. She had to fight back the emotions that threatened to engulf her. Somehow she had expected, or at least hoped for, his support. He had every right to challenge them, but he had given her no preparation for this. In some dim part of her memory his words 'I want what is best for you, no matter what you may think' echoed, but she could not believe that now. Nor did those words seem very real.

Ted frowned. 'These people have come forward because they found that when they sought justice, they received nothing but harassment. One voice alone can do little, but by joining a reform group, many private citizens feel they can make a difference; that when enough evidence is brought forth, government agencies can be reformed.'

The grilling continued as the words flew back and forth across the room, each time stronger, each time more harsh. The two male voices bit the air. Susan barely assimilated the words, but the intentions were unmistakable. To say she could hardly believe it was an understatement. And she sat stiff, formal, not showing that her stomach was lurching, that her skin burned, that it felt as if someone had taken a mallet to her temples. Why was Geoffrey trying to poke holes in their case? And they had only started. Geoffrey's attitude jolted her to the marrow of her bones.

All her arguments in favor of him were dashed in the time it took for him to fire his ammunition from the committee platform. Ted's words fired back, equally powerful, equally logical, but from a viewpoint as different as night from day. They were gladiators in an arena of ideas defining right and wrong.

Ted finished another question and deliberately turned his eyes to Chairman Smith as Geoffrey said, 'Thank you,' and leaned back in his chair. The interrogation was over — for the present.

Susan's jaw was clamped shut. She hoped Ted would continue to answer questions; she didn't trust herself to open her mouth. But then she took a long breath, silently. It wouldn't do to become angry. Not now. Afterward, in private, she would have a few things to say to Geoffrey Winston.

'Miss Franks.' Congressman Schilingham was looking at her. 'Can you clarify a point for me in the Jackson case?'

She snapped to attention and flipped the pages to the case he referred to. 'Yes,' she answered.

The thirty seconds it took him to ask the question were just enough time for her to gather her wits. She was nothing if not a professional. No one, not even Geoffrey Winston, could throw her off her stride in public.

She looked up and delivered her answer clearly and precisely. When Schilingham thanked her, she threw a glance of victory at Geoffrey. He was studying her, the antagonism gone, his look softer. But the anger still coursed in her blood, and she knew that the first moment she was able, an explosion would erupt from within her that would make Ted's Irish temper look like nothing.

'I think we've covered a great deal this morning,' Congressman Smith said. 'We will adjourn until after lunch.'

Just then Susan's eyes fell on Irwin Bradshaw, who had asked no questions at all. Something stirred in the back of her mind but failed to register clearly. She shuffled her papers into a folder and then hoisted her briefcase onto the table to shove the folder in.

Ted did the same with his light tan leather case. She noticed his outer calm but suspected that underneath he was as irritated by Geoffrey's questions as she was.

She turned to go out the door. A rumble in her stomach told her that she was hungry. But she was too keyed up to think about food. She supposed she would eat somewhere, but she felt an urge to leave the building rather than eat in the cafeteria on the first floor. She walked out the door and kept going down the long hallway to the elevator. Behind her, she could hear Ted acknowledge comments coming from some of the congressmen, and she had passed a reporter or two hanging around room 2255's door. Ted would talk to them. She didn't care much about their public image just now. It was a private affair she was thinking about.

She took the elevator down, passed through the glass doors and went down the steps and turned left. She barely heard the footsteps behind her, but she felt the light touch on her elbow as Geoffrey said, 'Susan.'

She turned and stared at him. Words were unnecessary. It was all too apparent that she thought he had some nerve to approach her as if nothing had happened.

He raised a hand. 'Susan, I want to explain.'

'You don't have to explain. You said everything in there quite plainly.' She jerked back. 'Now if you please, I have some things to do.'

He grasped her arm again, then turned his back on the Rayburn Building. 'Don't make a scene,' he said in a low voice. Then with a touch of humor, he added, 'Stop fuming. I much prefer the cool professional I saw inside.'

The nerve. But she turned and walked with him down the hill, saying under her breath, 'I won't make a scene, but it's not your feelings I'm sparing, it's my own reputation.'

He didn't speak as they continued down the slope of Capitol Hill. She didn't realize how quick their pace was until they broke their stride to cross the street. Her breathing was still ragged, but her head was clearing. The sun felt warm on her face, and as they passed a fountain and reflecting pool on their left, she slowed down a little. The lunch hour had brought other people out to enjoy the first warm day of spring. And it did her good to walk.

Finally, Geoffrey spoke. 'Will you have lunch with me?'

'No.' It was an instant reaction. She hadn't even decided where she would have lunch. Perhaps a hotdog from a street vendor would do. For a moment she glanced up at him, and his deep brown eyes held her gaze without rancor. The flutter of her heart made her even more angry. The love and the anger she bore him seemed to be one emotion that rippled out of her in all directions as if someone had thrown a penny in her own reflecting pool, shattering the calm surface. She said nothing but turned and walked on. He followed her.

'Susan.' he said, his voice more commanding. 'At least hear me out. I had a reason for doing what I did.'

She winced, feeling herself weaken, feeling herself acknowledge the feeling he created between them as if nothing else existed in the world except themselves. He took her elbow, and they continued toward the mall.

'Well,' he said, 'we've come this far. I suppose we might as well walk the rest of the way, though I had planned to take a taxi.'

'Where are we going?' It mattered little to her where they ate, just so they got it over with. He didn't answer but led her past the solid granite and marble buildings that sprawled at the foot of Capitol Hill.

She resented Geoffrey's attempt to make the AHG look bad. Of course, their certainty and their well-documented facts had prevented any slipups, and Ted thrived in battle, so to speak.

Where had Ted gotten to, she wondered. She had thought he had followed her out of the building and then she had been so startled at Geoffrey's approach that she had forgotten him.

She would have to calm down, she told herself. Fighting with Geoffrey would do no good. Perhaps he did have an explanation. Her reactions had left no room for any conclusion except that Geoffrey was challenging the AHG. What galled her was that he'd never so much as hinted that he would do that in public. His admonitions had come in the form of warnings. She had believed him to be on their side even though Ted didn't. That was what hurt, she realized. She had trusted him.

The angry crushed feeling still resided in her chest, and she felt the threat of grief ready to spill over. Imbecile, she told herself. She should never have gotten on such intimate terms with Geoffrey Winston. Ted was right. She should have listened to him.

Geoffrey still strode purposefully along the sidewalk. 'Where are we going?' she asked again, her feet beginning to tire and her stomach beginning to growl in earnest.

'My favorite cafeteria,' he said.

Susan's brows lifted, and her mouth opened as he led her across the street and escorted her to the modern-looking marble-and-glass building that housed the National Air and Space Museum, part of the Smithsonian. Her eyes widened even further when he steered her toward the entrance.

'I like the cafeteria upstairs,' he said as they passed through the doors and into the spacious interior, with missiles pointing skyward and a piece of the moon on display.

'Well, so do I,' she said, and gave up trying to understand. She was familiar with the cafeteria, with its windows that looked out in three directions. She just hadn't thought of coming to the museum specifically to eat here. But why not? She never thought of congressmen eating here, either, only tourists, but again, why not?

That was her problem, she realized. She couldn't seem to separate Geoffrey Winston the congressman from Geoffrey Winston the man. Where was the dividing line? She had foolishly thought she could have a relationship with the man, pushing his public image aside. But that would never be possible. He was what he stood for in public.

Once inside the cafeteria, Susan gripped the tray Geoffrey handed her in one hand, still carrying her briefcase in the other, and walked to the food carousel.

After they had made their selections, they

chose a table by the window in the dining room. Susan could see the domed roof of the National Archives across the mall, and a pang went through her as she remembered their chance meeting there. Voices droned, and trays rattled, but they had no trouble hearing each other over the lunchtime din. Susan gazed at him, hating the way her heart turned over when she looked at his strong features.

'Well,' she said finally, 'you were going to explain.'

He took a sip of coffee, then said, 'Yes. I see where your evidence is leading, and it frightens me.'

'So?'

'You are obviously going to say that someone within Globenet is using their data banks to circulate false reports about private citizens.'

'It is the conclusion we hope the subcommittee will reach.'

He spoke lower now, leaning toward her. 'I don't like it, Susan.'

'What do you mean by that?'

'There's something amiss, something left out.'

'You seemed to imply that at the hearing. Why bring it up again? Is this what you mean by explaining?'

He stared intently at her. 'The important

thing is why would anyone do that? I don't think you realize you're up against some very powerful men, and you don't know their reasons for the cover-up.'

She bristled. 'Well, they're going to be exposed. At least we hope our hearing will lead Congress to a full-scale investigation into Globenet's operations. Perhaps they're covering up a large conspiracy of some kind.'

'Perhaps they are. But if so, then you're in very great danger.'

She shivered, remembering the prowler at her window. But surely so silly a prank was not the product of sophisticated criminals, if indeed that was whom they were up against.

Geoffrey went on. 'I think that someone is going to prevent this subcommittee from arriving at the conclusion you want it to reach and that the recommendations you hope for will never be made.'

'You seem to be the only person in that room stopping us.'

'I told you, I had a reason.'

She simply stared at him, waiting for his explanation.

'Susan, did it ever occur to you that I am playing devil's advocate simply to draw the enemy out?'

'No. I must say it never did.'

'Well, give it some thought. And I'm still

not sure where Ted Branagan fits into this.'

She pulled her mouth back in an expression of irony.

'Susan, I think that someone connected to Globenet is watching your activities very carefully. I wouldn't be surprised if they've planted someone in your organization, as well.'

'But who?'

He didn't answer. He obviously still thought it was Ted — that Ted was really working for the other side, but that was impossible.

'Susan you'll never get away with what you're trying to do — blow apart Globenet's network.'

'Why not? How will they stop us?'

'Any number of ways. Threats, stolen evidence, sabotage. Tell me, has anything at all unusual happened to you since you undertook interviewing people for today's hearings?'

She looked down. She hadn't told him about the prowler or about the break-in at the office. She and Ted had decided they probably had no connection with their investigations. Nothing confidential had been stolen from their files. And what could anyone hope to accomplish by staring in her window? Then another thought occurred to her. Perhaps the two incidents were related and someone wanted to confuse and frighten her.

She put her fingers to her temples in a gesture of fatigue. 'What would you have me do?'

He made a move as if to touch her, then seemed to think better of it until he had won her trust again. 'I just want you to take some precautions.'

'Such as?' If he asked her to give up her work, the relationship was definitely over. She would not see him again. She braced herself for what he had to say.

'I rather wish you weren't living alone,' he said.

She let out her breath. 'Is that all?'

'For now, yes. I would feel better if you stayed with someone else.'

In spite of herself, something in her responded to his concern. 'I would feel silly, frightened into leaving my own apartment.'

'I know it sounds melodramatic. But, Susan, if some serious attempt is made to stop you from presenting your evidence or from doing further research, I'd never forgive myself.' The look of concern he gave her threatened to melt her last reserves. She suddenly sensed that he was as confused about their situation as she. He, too, must be fighting opposing forces within himself.

'I suppose I knew there was an element of danger when I took this job,' she said. 'That is, I didn't realize it at first, but when you stir up trouble, I guess you ought to expect trouble in return.' She lowered her gaze. 'Anyway, I've got to face whatever comes as a result of what we're doing.'

'But you don't have to face it alone.'

She skirted his implications. 'Our main defense is that the law is on our side. In fact, that's what we're trying to prove. That crime doesn't pay.'

Geoffrey tightened his jaw. 'I know. I stand for the very thing you speak of. But you and I both know that the world is not an ideal place. The criminals you fight are behind the scenes. They may never be caught.'

'The first job is to find out why they're circulating false reports — find out what illicit activities of their own they're covering up by doing so.'

'That's just what I'm afraid of, for your sake.'

'Why for my sake?'

'Because if their own activities are important enough to them, they'll go to any lengths to protect them.'

She swallowed. What he said was true. But she had gone too far. She couldn't turn back now. She sighed. 'It's a moot point, isn't it? We've got the evidence. We can't turn our backs on it.'

He picked up his coffee cup, saw that it was empty and put it down. 'Look, I know I can't dissuade you. All I can do is try to assess where the opposition lies.'

Susan studied him. Up until now she had been so sure he was trying to discourage them that she never thought he might actually be onto something they might be able to use, something he wasn't telling her. What if he actually knew whom the AHG was up against and simply hadn't told them?

'Geoffrey, do you know something that — if I knew, it would make a difference?'

'If I knew anything for sure, I would tell you.' He shook his head. 'All I have is suspicion. No more facts than you do.'

'Then why this air of secrecy?' she asked.

'Policy. I never say anything I can't prove. I have my suspicions, it's true, but I don't like to tarnish someone's reputation unless I have proof.'

'But you've already warned me about Ted. It's the same thing, isn't it?'

His eyes narrowed slightly when she mentioned Ted's name. 'Yes, I admit I have reason not to trust him.'

'Then if you have reason, tell me.'

Geoffrey sighed. 'Ted's activities before he joined the AHG. You said you didn't know exactly what he did.'

'No, only that he studied for a graduate degree for three years and traveled in Europe. Oh, and he worked on the *Village Voice* in New York for a few years.'

'And then he seized on the AHG as being his true calling in life.'

'Yes.'

Geoffrey seemed to look at the pictures in his mind as if he were assessing some facts. 'He's always been interested in helping his country, you say?'

'Yes, why?'

'I have reason to think that Ted was at one time connected with the very people he seems to be fighting now. I just want to be sure.'

Her mouth dropped open, and she felt suddenly cold all over. Ted, a fraud? 'I don't believe it.'

'I knew you wouldn't. That's why I didn't say anything for so long. And I want to do some more checking. I'm not sure myself. I only learned that there might be a possible connection. His name turned up on a confidential list of informers.'

'Informers?' The room swayed. The idea that Ted himself might be setting the AHG up to fight a losing battle was so fraught with

172

contradictions that her mind simply would not accept it. 'No, no,' she was saying. 'Not Ted.'

Geoffrey gave her such a look of despair and longing that she opened her mouth to speak but found she was unable to respond.

'Susan, my love,' he almost whispered. 'I only hope that someday I see in your face the same loyalty and defense of me if anyone ever challenges me as I see in your face for Ted Branagan. It's a very admirable quality.'

She slumped against the back of her seat. He was right. It was awkward. Susan seemed to have automatic responses about Ted built in. She had been so sure of him. But now the man she thought she was falling in love with was casting doubt on the beacon of her course. Surely not just out of petty jealousy. Geoffrey Winston was a mature man and didn't have to play petty games.

Something wrenched in her heart, and she longed for this trial to be over. She longed to reach across the table and smooth the worry lines in Geoffrey's face. She wanted to lose herself in those eyes that seemed to express such deep emotions, caressing her face with his glance.

He watched her, and she could see the gratitude in his eyes when she finally took his hand and returned his squeeze. 'Geoffrey,' she said. It was a plea. 'If you really want to help me, tell me what you want me to do.' She still wasn't sure she could do whatever he asked.

His face relaxed slightly, as if the battle were half over. 'I want you to move in with someone you trust.'

She knit her brows. 'I hate to run away like this, but if you really think I should, I suppose I could go stay with my aunt in the suburbs. I could still drive in to work. Of course I couldn't stay there indefinitely.'

'I'll want the address, of course.'

'After the hearing today, then, I'll call her.' It was such a small thing, but she would do it if it would make him happy, would put his mind at rest.

'All right.' They rose to go.

Rather than hiking back to the Rayburn Building, the way they had come, they hailed a taxi on Independence Avenue in front of the museum. Susan pondered her relationship with Geoffrey as they rode up the hill. Things certainly weren't settled yet, not by a long shot, but there was a sort of truce between them, she felt. Meanwhile, there was a job to be done.

When they returned to the hearing chambers, Ted at once approached. 'Where — ' His eye caught the movement of Congressman

Winston following her into the room. 'Oh, I see.' His face turned a dark shade of red, and he busied himself with his papers as they seated themselves.

'Ted,' she said, but couldn't think of a plausible explanation with others close enough to overhear them. Susan prayed her face didn't show the turbulent emotions inside her. She would have to deal with Ted later.

The afternoon session went well. All of the committee members had questions, which Susan and Ted answered smoothly. She was distracted by Irwin Bradshaw's penetrating stare a time or two, and she was looking at him when Ernest Smith said, 'As you have pointed out, the one agency that has access to all the law-enforcement agencies, including the files of our own intelligence organizations, is Globenet.' Was she imagining it, or did Bradshaw's eyes narrow as Globenet was mentioned?

Ted was quick to acknowledge Congressman Smith. 'You are correct, Mr. Smith. Globenet does have access through the Treasury Enforcement Communication System to the files of the U.S. Customs Bureau, the FBI's National Crime Information Center, the IRS Intelligence Division, IRS Inspection Service and other bureaus. Through TECS,

Globenet communicates with twenty thousand local and state law-enforcement agencies and places nationwide lookouts.'

'It stands to reason,' said Smith, 'that Globenet's operations need to be scrutinized to see if the false reports may have originated there, or at least find out why they continued to be transmitted through Globenet's channels. We have a responsibility to see what our taxpayers get for U.S. involvement with that organization.'

'Yes, sir, it stands to reason,' answered Ted.

Susan's spine tingled. They were picking up the bait. She glanced at Geoffrey. He, too, was watching Bradshaw, and then his eyes slid to Smith in speculation. Susan raised her brows. She could see by Geoffrey's look that he was pleasantly surprised.

Congressman Smith cleared his throat. 'I suggest we adjourn until tomorrow at ten A.M. It will give us some time to digest the information we have covered. Further questions will be raised at that time. Thank you all for your attention. And thank you, Miss Franks and Mr. Branagan, for your considerable efforts on behalf of the AHG.'

Susan nodded as Ted said, 'Thank you.' The meeting was adjourned.

She looked down and gathered her papers together, sensing the tension as Ted stood to leave. She wanted to say something to him. They ought to leave together. She wasn't planning to leave with Geoffrey.

Ted was already walking out the door when she caught up to him. 'It went rather well, don't you think?'

'As well as I expected.'

'Ted, don't rush. I'm coming with you.'

He turned and gave her a quizzical look. 'Are you?'

'Of course.'

He shrugged and led the way to the elevator and out the door of the building, as if he didn't care whether she followed or not. He set such a fast pace up the hill, she nearly had to run to keep up.

Out of breath and exasperated, Susan grabbed Ted by the arm to stop him. She turned him toward her and looked at him, hoping to see some grain of compassion in his emerald eyes. When she had caught her breath, she said, 'Ted, please let's not part this way.'

He said nothing but stood looking at her, waiting for her to make the next move.

'I want you to know my plans. I'm going to stay with my Aunt Emily for a while.'

'Why?' he asked in surprise.

'Oh, I don't know. I haven't seen her in a long time,' Susan said, avoiding the real reason — as she'd found herself doing more and more with Ted lately.

He zeroed in on her, though. 'You're not getting scared of anything, are you, Susan?'

She shrugged. 'Well, it can't hurt to stay there.'

Ted studied her. 'Susan, you've got to tell me why you're doing this. The issues we're dealing with are a bit sensational, of course, but you knew when you started — '

She cut him off. 'It's partly that, yes. But I really haven't seen her much.'

'Well,' he said, his eyes still grilling her, 'I suppose it's a good idea.'

She looked down, feeling sheepish. She'd never run from anything before. Was that what she was doing now — or was it simply because she wanted to appease Geoffrey?

7

Susan pulled up in front of her aunt's neat little brick house at the end of a cul-de-sac. The lawn looked freshly mowed, and bright white paint adorned the trim. The smell of honeysuckle, faint in the city, was stronger here. Aunt Emily, who was only ten years older than Susan, prided herself on her housekeeping. For Emily, life had taken an easy course, until two years ago when Uncle Jason had died.

She had been overjoyed at the prospect of Susan staying with her for a while. 'I've gotten used to living alone,' she had said when Susan phoned, 'but it's not really very much fun. I'd love to have you, and you can stay as long as you like.'

Susan parked next to her aunt's blue Datsun and got out. She walked around to look at her back left bumper. It was dented, and some paint was scratched off at the side of the car, as well.

'What a waste of time,' she muttered under her breath. She cursed the driver who had caused this little fender bender on her way here. A black Sunbird had grazed her as she'd turned onto the highway from a side street. He'd been behind her and had followed her onto the highway and bumped her from behind. Then he'd driven away before she had a chance to get his license number.

Susan had pulled over to look at the damage, but there was nothing she could do, so she'd continued on her trip.

As she was standing there, Emily came out to meet her, and Susan smiled a greeting at the young-looking thirty-nine-year-old dressed in designer jeans and a long-sleeved man's work shirt. Her short brown hair was pushed back under a bandanna scarf, and hoop earrings hung from her earlobes.

'Good to see you, Emily,' said Susan, kissing her aunt's cheek. Emily had the same thinness of face as her niece, and Susan thought she'd gotten more attractive as she grew older. There was an unassuming poise about her that Susan admired.

'What happened here?' asked Emily, looking at the dent.

Susan gave a rueful look, raking her dark hair back over her ear in frustration. 'A guy bumped me as I was coming here. He wasn't watching where he was going, I guess. He didn't even stop.'

'You weren't hurt, were you?' asked Emily.

Susan shook her head. 'Oh, no, just angry,

you know. It'll probably eat up my deductible.'

'Well, I'm sorry, Susan. Here, let me take your bag. We'll try to make your evening more pleasant, so you can take your mind off it. You can't do anything about it tonight.'

'You'll never change, Emily.' She meant it as a compliment. Emily loved to entertain, and Susan could tell her aunt meant to pamper her. Well, it might be a pleasure to let someone take care of her just a little bit, as unused to it as she was.

Inside the house, Susan followed her aunt up a flight of carpeted stairs to a guest bedroom with windows overlooking the backyard and an arboretum behind it.

'I've always loved this view,' Susan said, peeking through the venetian blinds at the sea of green behind the house.

Emily had placed the bag on the bed. 'Shall I help you unpack?'

'No, thanks, Em. I'll just throw some things on hangers. And the room looks lovely.' Percale sheets were turned down over a quilted coverlet, and fresh-cut chrysanthemums stood in a crystal vase on the night table. The pale blue of the room was picked up in the coverlet and the linen doilies on the bureau and dressing table. A far cry from her apartment, she thought, shaking her head.

Somehow housekeeping had never been very high on Susan's list of priorities.

'You make yourself comfortable, then come down when you're ready. Have you eaten?'

'No, not really.'

'Good, there's plenty for both of us. I waited until you got here to eat.' She surveyed the room as if to make sure everything was perfect.

'Thanks, Em. I guess food does sound good. Especially your cooking.' *Especially after a cafeteria lunch*, she thought.

They laughed and talked through dinner, and Susan began to feel like a real guest, forgetting her troubles. After dinner they dragged out old photo albums and struggled to identify people who had been with them at family reunions in Texas. Susan smiled over pictures of herself as a teenager and a college student.

'But Emily, I don't look like that anymore.'

Emily studied her face for a moment. 'No,' she said thoughtfully, 'you don't.'

Susan looked at the smiling brown eyes, the creamy skin with a trace of plumpness about her in the pictures. She was thinner now. And she had lines about the corners of her mouth and shadows under her eyes that she had to cover with makeup.

My life isn't like that anymore, either, she

thought silently, turning another page in the album, realizing how carefree she'd been as a student. Oh, she'd always rallied behind causes, but being young, there wasn't so much responsibility attached to what she did. At ten o'clock, she and Emily began to put the pictures away.

'I'd better go up,' she said to Emily. 'I've got some things to review before tomorrow's hearing.'

'Important doings, is it?'

'Well, we think so.'

Emily stood and looked down at her niece. 'Susan, you know I love having you here. But you didn't say why you wanted to come. You don't have to tell me if you don't want to.'

Susan wasn't sure how much to say. But she couldn't get away with less than the truth with her aunt, and she knew it. 'It's a bit complicated. I met a man.' She looked down, trying to frame her thoughts.

'Oh?' She could hear the interest in Emily's voice.

'Yes, you see, he's concerned about the investigation we're doing at the AHG. He told me he didn't want me staying alone.' There, it was out. She continued. 'I guess it wasn't very fair of me to come out here, was it? I mean Geoffrey, that's his name, thinks we might be threatened or something.' She shook her head. Guilt assailed her as she realized that she might be bringing trouble to her aunt. Only she had been so sure there wouldn't be any trouble.

A fleeting image of the car that had hit her came into her mind, but she discounted it. That had only been an unfortunate accident, possibly a drunken driver. Things like that happened all the time in the congested area around D.C.

'Well, then it's a darned good thing you came,' said Emily. 'Most sensible thing you've done since you were a little child. Whoever this Geoffrey is, he sounds like he's got a head on his shoulders.'

Susan broke into a smile. 'That he does.' She was relieved that her aunt thought she had done the right thing. The last thing she wanted was to cause anyone, especially a loved one, trouble.

'How's your boss — Ted, isn't it?'

Susan frowned. 'Oh, he's all right.' She needn't describe the going-over Ted had given her when she'd told him she was coming here.

Emily moved about, picking up the albums and returning them to the cabinet where she kept them.

'Like anything before you go up?'

Susan shook her head. 'No, thanks, Em.'

She smiled again. 'I'm glad I'm here.'

'Me, too.'

★ ★ ★

The next morning Susan rose early so she could enjoy sitting on the sun deck overlooking the backyard for a while before she drove in for the day's session of the hearing. Emily, clad in the same jeans but a lavender T-shirt this time, was already puttering in the kitchen.

'Coffee's hot,' she said when Susan came in.

'Thanks, I'll have some. Care to sit on the deck with me for a while?'

'In a minute. I want to get this bread in the oven.'

Susan took her cup and opened the sliding-glass door, then closed it behind her. She breathed in the sweet air and took a seat in a canvas deck chair, feasting her eyes on low-hanging sycamore and dogwood trees. The arboretum behind the house stretched as far as the eye could see. She leaned back in her chair, relaxing.

It would be so easy to give it all up. She could have a quiet life, like her aunt, who lived mostly on her husband's insurance and a part-time job. She could study. But that was the hitch. Whatever she studied would lead her to . . .

No, it would never work. She had once met a private investigator who said, 'Once a spook, always a spook,' and it was a bit like that with her. Though she wasn't a spy, she had a nose for investigating facts, researching old musty, dusty secrets, but secrets nonetheless. She was in deep, she realized as she breathed the warmth from her coffee cup. She doubted she could ever really give it up.

Finally, Emily came out to join her. 'It's peaceful here,' Susan said, shading her eyes from the sunlight that was now slanting directly through the trees.

'Yes,' said Emily. 'I like it here. I've spent untold hours on this deck, just thinking.'

Susan wondered if she still mourned Jason. 'You seem to have a busy life.'

Emily took a sip of coffee and put her feet on the canvas chair opposite. 'I keep busy. Jason left me well enough off. The part-time job is just enough to give me ready cash. I have everything I want.' She looked directly at Susan. 'Except Jason, of course.'

'Do you still miss him?'

She looked out over the yard, where a robin tugged at a worm. 'I'll go on missing him. But it's a dull ache now. You manage to fill up your life with other things. And his spirit lives on — somewhere.'

Susan thought of Geoffrey. How wonderful it must be to have such a close relationship with someone, to be able to go on loving them and knowing that their spirit dwelled somewhere after they died. Then she steered her thoughts away from that territory. It was too early in the morning for such heavy thoughts.

But she knew that Emily had had something with Jason that she had not yet found. Even with her newfound feelings for Geoffrey Winston, Susan knew that their relationship lacked something. Trust. Because they were both caught in the morass of issues and intrigue, there had been no room for trust to grow. Suddenly she wished with all her heart that she and Geoffrey could be just two ordinary people. But that was impossible. She had just concluded that she was not ordinary and never would be. And Geoffrey wasn't, either. They were two birds of a feather. Was that why they were so attracted to each other? She felt she was on the way to finding some answers about her confused feelings. But she couldn't quite grasp them yet. She needed more time.

Susan roused herself and went upstairs to finish getting ready. Even now she would have to fight traffic going into the city.

The day's session went off successfully. In spite of Geoffrey's warnings, the subcommittee resolved to look into the history and operation of Globenet, seeing in it the potential for abuse of the rights of private citizens. Suddenly Congress was aware that nobody in government appeared to know anything about the purpose or structure of the international organization or of its relation to the many diverse governments that supported it. But it was apparent that Globenet had access to the police intelligence files of most of the Western world and that the data was interchangeable between member countries. And there were no checks on security from any other body on the data being interchanged. The potential for false reports was great, as private citizens had little access to the data being exchanged about them.

★ ★ ★

Phase two of Operation Globenet, as the AHG staff came to call it, was more research. Congress was conducting a full-scale investigation with their own staff, but if the AHG came up with additional findings, they would testify before another subcommittee. Ted had suggested that Susan study Globenet's history from its founding in 1935.

Susan remained at Emily's and drove into the city to work. She left at seven every morning to avoid traffic and opened up the office. She usually had an hour to herself before the others showed up, when she was free to go to the libraries or other agencies in which she sought information for their cases. She would finish by four o'clock and try to beat the traffic to the suburbs. Geoffrey had gone back to New Mexico to do some necessary work there. When they had said goodbye, she had tried to reassure him that there was nothing to worry about.

But she remembered the look of concern in his eyes as he said, 'I hope you're right. I only wish I didn't have to make this trip.'

She had teased him. 'I'm not even living at home. What more do you want? I could get a watchdog.'

His eyes had flickered. 'Yes,' he said. 'I'd thought of that.' Then they had changed the subject.

Ted's conversations with Susan were shorter these days. He no longer offered to brainstorm with her. But at least she had Emily to talk to, and for that she was grateful.

Susan sipped coffee from a Styrofoam cup and looked over the papers on her desk. There had been no more citizens' complaints about false reports. Could that be because of the hearing? If so, then perhaps they'd succeeded in scaring Globenet off. Of course, even Globenet would have trouble suppressing all their own false reports once they got into the system. Once in the data banks and disseminated to law-enforcement agencies, they were like runaway snowballs, she imagined. She pulled the corner of her mouth in a wry expression. That was mixing metaphors.

She studied the statements of the people they'd interviewed just prior to the hearing. Now that the AHG had gotten Congress's attention, they had time to analyze more carefully the statements of citizens who'd complained before. What Susan and her colleagues wanted to know was why these individuals had been singled out. At first, Susan had assumed the false-reports victims were just random cases. That was possible, but it was more likely that these people had either done something to offend Globenet officials, or else they happened to have a set of circumstances convenient for Globenet's use. Either way, they still seemed to be innocent victims. The AHG staff hoped that by an analysis of cases, a pattern would form, thus leading them closer to Globenet's motives.

Susan studied Ted obliquely from her desk. This morning he was on the phone with the New York chapter. They were coming up with some hot material, and she could see the flush of color rising up the back of Ted's neck. He was onto something.

Geoffrey had suggested that Ted had in some way been connected with their adversaries. What adversaries? Globenet? Others in power who manipulated criminal dossiers? Even if he had, he couldn't still be under their influence, Susan thought — surely not.

But she had to satisfy herself, to find out if there was any basis for Geoffrey's allegations. When Ted finished the call, he hunched over his desk, pencil in hand. Then he looked up, as if he had felt her stare.

'What is it?' he asked.

'Oh, I was just thinking.' She glanced at Cindy, typing a report. Michael was noisily rearranging one of the interview rooms. Ted followed her gaze, then returned his glance to her.

'Uh,' she said, 'why don't we get a bite after we close up here?'

His eyebrows lifted in surprise. 'If you like.'

'Sure. I could fill you in on my research. I think I've got a good lead, and I'd like to know what you think about it.'

'Okay. Whatever you say.'

After the others had gone, Susan and Ted locked important documents in the filing cabinets and left. Susan felt troubled as she led the way down the hall to the elevator. It wouldn't be easy to bring up what was on her mind.

They decided to eat in Georgetown so Susan could pick up her mail and some clothes at her apartment.

Ted waited in her living room while she changed into more comfortable clothes. As she came out of the bedroom, he was leaning with one arm propped against the window frame, looking intently at the street below. He turned, and for a moment they eyed each other. Then she said, 'Ted, I want to ask you something.' She walked to her worktable and ran her fingers across the library binding of a book that lay there. He moved away from the window.

'You've never told me everything you did before you joined the AHG. What made you seek it out?'

He pulled his mouth back in a sardonic expression. 'Why the third degree all of a sudden?'

She fiddled with the back of the chair next to the table. 'It's not the third degree. It's just that we've known each other for some time, and we've never really talked

192

about why you joined the AHG in the first place.'

'So? The congressman turning your head around again? Making you wonder about your friends?'

She opened her mouth to protest, but she couldn't deny it. 'Ted, don't make it sound like that. You're my closest friend. Nothing anyone could say would change that. I just got to wondering what you used to be like, what made you want to get into government reform.'

'You know, Susan, you'd make a terrible spy. You don't just come out and ask your enemy for information point-blank.'

She couldn't resist a wry grin. 'It would save a lot of time.'

He grinned at her joke, and the tension eased a bit. 'I'll tell you what you want to know while we eat,' he said.

'All right.' She picked up her bag, and they left for Georgetown Park to get sandwiches.

Ted's description of his philosophy and outlook on life before he knew her contained nothing that would prove Geoffrey's allegations. She already knew about his graduate studies at Colorado University, and he added a few amusing anecdotes about traveling in Europe and working at the *Village Voice* that made her laugh. By the end of the evening they were almost on the same footing as before. And when he walked her back to the garage where her car was parked, she could sense the old camaraderie.

She turned to say good-bye, and for a moment he leaned close to her.

'Thanks for dinner. I enjoyed it,' she said.

'Yes,' he said, studying her. Only the diffused light from a street lamp at the corner cast a faint illumination on her face. She smiled, then looked at him with a puzzled expression as he seemed about to say something. But he appeared to change his mind and opened the door of her car. 'See you tomorrow,' he said.

She thought she detected a trace of wistfulness in his voice — unlike the Ted she knew.

After he had gone, she drove slowly through the city, pondering this new side of Ted she hadn't known before. She was so used to seeing him always keyed up, always hot on the trail of something, she didn't know what to make of the vulnerability he seemed to be revealing lately. She shook her head. She didn't know why he was displaying it, especially now.

★   ★   ★

Susan spent Sunday at the office, since Geoffrey was still out of town. She had toyed with the idea of staying home and doing some gardening with Emily, but there were summary reports to be written. She had had a wonderful relaxing day at the house Saturday, and she felt refreshed.

She arrived at noon and worked until about three, when she went out for a coffee break and to get some sun. Capitol Hill was quiet. She loved the city when there was no bustle, and she could stroll along the walks with other Sunday idlers. She returned to the office about four and worked steadily until eight o'clock.

When she stopped typing on Cindy's typewriter, she was aware of the silence around her. Night had fallen, and with it came an even more prevailing stillness. She decided to quit. The work was done, anyway. She was just typing up some notes for the staff meeting tomorrow. Tonight she would relax with a book at home.

She rolled the chair back, stood and bent over to stretch the small of her back where tension had gathered after sitting for such a long time. Then with a groan of relief, as she felt the rigid muscles loosen, she went to the coat closet to fetch her linen jacket. She took her briefcase with her, just out of habit.

She double-checked the locked filing cabinets, swept her eye around the office and went to the door. She swung it open, and before she could turn out the light switch, she drew up short. The hallway outside was dark. The bulbs must have burned out.

Leaving the office light on, she shut the door and locked it. She was barely able to see the lock by the light that escaped from the crack below the door and the streetlight shining through the window at the far end of the hall. Then she felt her way along the wall to the elevator.

She stood in the dark, listening to her own breathing as the elevator creaked its way to her floor. Finally, it came, and the doors slowly opened. She was about to step in when movement at the end of the hall caught her attention. She glanced that way, startled. For a moment so brief she wasn't sure she really saw it, the figure of a man was silhouetted against the window. He was large, and he appeared to be wearing a raincoat. Then he was gone, vanished into the shadows.

She stepped quickly into the elevator, her heart thudding in hard, insistent beats. She pushed the button marked One, and the slow downward motion began. In her pocket she fingered the key to the glass door at the front of the building, which would be locked at this hour.

The elevator stopped, but the doors did not open. Then the light above her head went out. From the sudden silence that enveloped her, she realized the electric power had failed. And the elevator did not budge. The minutes culminated in a grip of terror as she clenched her fists and banged on the doors that imprisoned her. But only absolute stillness and darkness greeted her.

She stepped to her right, feeling along the panel for an alarm button. She tried to remember the sequence of buttons, pressing each one in turn. But nothing happened. She was trapped.

Think, she told herself as the panic threatened to seize her. Where was she? Between three and two? How long had she been in the elevator before it had stopped? She had thought she was nearly to the ground floor. But then she always anticipated it too soon.

What had happened? A power failure? Surely no one had done this deliberately. The hideous thought forced its way into her mind. No, she argued, a power failure was a common thing, and she had seen mainten-ance men working on the elevator only this week. If they were maintenance men . . . But then what about the shadowy figure at the end of the hall?

She tried to control the hammering of her heart. She couldn't stay here all night. Emily would begin to wonder — if she stayed awake. She knew Susan often came in late and didn't usually wait up.

She sobbed as she bent her knees and sank to the floor. She felt the walls closing in and tried to fight off the claustrophobia. She never liked being in small enclosures. Was there no one to help her?

She whispered a futile cry. 'Help.' It would be useless if she screamed. No one would come. She was the only one in the building, and the alarm bell seemed to be disconnected.

Then she heaved herself up again and pounded her fists against the panel of buttons. 'Work! Work!' she demanded. Finally giving up, she slid to the floor again, her hands running down the cold metal.

She lay there, taking deep breaths. There seemed to be enough air for her to breathe. At least she wouldn't suffocate.

Then she remembered that most elevators had exits through the ceiling. If she could get out into the elevator shaft . . .

She stood up and reached, her fingertips missing the ceiling by inches, she judged in the darkness. She might be able to stand on her briefcase. But it was hopeless. Even if she could reach the ceiling, she wouldn't be able to pull herself up. Besides, in the darkness of the elevator shaft there would be no place to go unless she could reach the doors to one of the floors and force them open.

She positioned the case on end and placed a foot on it. It rocked, and she moved it nearer the wall so that she could stand without falling. One foot, then the other. Then she reached again. Her hand touched cold metal. But nothing more.

Another stretch. But she couldn't discern any opening, and she toppled to the floor with a cry, her fists hitting the floor in anger. 'Damn it,' she cried. 'Why?'

Then she collapsed. She groped for her jacket and pulled it around her. She was stuck here for the night. She huddled next to her briefcase, the jacket up over her shoulders, trying not to think of the hours she would pass here. She leaned against the wall and shut her eyes, willing the panic to subside, waiting for time to pass.

Her muscles refused to relax, and images continued to pass through her mind. She tried to even out her breathing. Finally — she didn't know how many hours later — she fell into a restless sleep. Still the images persisted: terrible faces haunting her, congressmen throwing questions at her, Irwin Bradshaw with his lowered lids, Geoffrey trying to help her and Ted smirking in the distance.

8

Geoffrey Winston walked through the sliding-glass doors onto his redwood sun deck. The sun was rising over the Sandia Mountains, and he had not slept most of the night. He had been deeply concerned about what he learned yesterday afternoon and had sat up late last night reading statistics and miscellaneous data his staff had gathered on the origins and history of Globenet. And he didn't like what he'd read.

If such information was so easy to obtain, why wasn't it more publicly known? In the mid-seventies, newspapers in Britain and West Germany reported that Globenet was being sued for circulating false reports from their secret files. But since it came on the heels of Watergate, the story attracted little notice in the United States. Of course, public knowledge and publicity were two different things, Geoffrey well knew. The amount of publicity an issue got usually had little to do with the righteousness of the issue.

One thing made him curious, though. If Globenet was a private organization, begun in France before World War II, why was it using government space in Washington? The agency did not have power to make arrests, only to foster the exchange of information between various police forces.

Geoffrey strode to the living room and walked around the room, still thinking. As he made a tour of the place, he thought of Susan. She would like it here. He could picture her sitting on the stone hearth in front of the fireplace or there, next to the grand piano.

He thought of calling her, but it was too early. He really should concentrate on the matter at hand, and so he brought his attention back to Globenet. The U.S. government paid half a million dollars a year for U.S. membership in Globenet, and what did the taxpayers get for it? He felt as if he were looking at several disparate pieces of a puzzle. If he had the missing piece, they might all fall together.

A picture of Susan came into his mind again, and with it a feeling of warmth and longing. How he wanted these investigations to be over. He shook his head. What was he going to do about Susan? He had no doubt that he wanted to make her his wife, but he couldn't live with the anxiety he felt with her snooping into matters that were too big for her to handle. What could he say to convince her? In order for her to give up the type of investigative work she did, he would have to think of something to replace it, something that would satisfy her — and challenge her. He knew she didn't consider her research activities investigation, but it amounted to the same thing. By digging far enough into someone's or something's past, she could turn up secrets the parties being investigated didn't want known, and that's what the AHG was beginning to do.

He went back to the kitchen, saw that the coffee maker had done its job and poured himself a cup. Thursday he would board a flight back to Washington. Thank God. He still had business to take care of here in his district, but all the time he was like a horse pulling at the bit, wanting to head for home. A smile tugged at his lips. He used to consider Albuquerque home, not Washington. Now it was the other way around.

The April light began to filter into the house, and he sipped his coffee, watching dust particles dance in the slanted beams of sun. Today was Sunday, and aside from some paperwork and reading, he couldn't really do much until his staff came in tomorrow. He would do something outdoors, even though he knew his mind wouldn't be on it. He shook his head. He was tired of holding up the burden alone. He needed someone beside him. Susan, to be exact. He thought of her soft curling dark hair, her sculptured face, the way she looked when she was asleep, when she didn't know he was watching her. He smiled to himself, choking down the coffee and trying to shut off the arousal he felt. He would save that for a time when it could be fulfilled. Thursday night, he hoped.

★   ★   ★

When Cindy Conrad arrived for work Monday morning, she discovered the night's power failure and called the building manager. He came and got the power back on as several other tenants of the building began to arrive. When the elevator doors opened, Cindy gasped. Susan was struggling to her feet, rubbing her eyes, her hair tangled around her face.

'My God, Susan. What happened?' said Cindy, going white. Just then Ted arrived. Elbowing his way through the crowd, he went up to Susan.

Slowly she oriented herself. She was aware of her cramped muscles, and there was Ted, hovering about her, and Cindy, looking as if she'd seen a ghost. Then Susan remembered. She clutched at Ted's arms. The fears came back, and she thought she would start to babble. But the sight of a dozen people around her forced her to get a grip on her sanity.

'Let her have some air,' Ted said, helping her out of the elevator. The crowd stepped back.

Cindy stood dumbfounded, still pale. 'Is she all right?' she asked, finally. 'Susan, what happened?'

'I — ' Her throat was dry. 'Worked yesterday. Was alone. The power went out. Can I have some water?'

'I'll get it.' Cindy looked about, realizing there wasn't a water fountain on the main floor. She looked questioningly at Susan and Ted. 'I'll have to go upstairs for it, I guess.'

'Do you want to go up?' Ted asked Susan. But as she stared at the small prison, her stomach turned over.

'No,' she said in a faint tone. 'I want out.'

Ted led her outside, where she squinted in the sunlight. But the air was fresh, and soon she felt stronger.

'Cindy went to bring the water. She'll come back here.'

'It's all right.' Susan could swallow now. She took a few steps. Everything on the street looked so normal — the stores, the brightly painted Victorian row houses across the street

205

with their uneven brick sidewalk in front. And yet she had just passed a night of horror.

'The elevator?' she asked.

He shrugged. 'Must have been a fuse. The janitor turned the circuit breaker back on. You okay?'

She nodded. 'But the alarm button. I pushed it. It didn't ring.'

He frowned. 'Probably wasn't anybody in the building Sunday night to answer it even if it had. Still . . . '

'Ted, do you think — ' She left the question unfinished.

He looked down the street. 'I don't know what to think. Why were you working alone, anyway?'

She shook her head. 'I know. I can't seem to get it through my head that we're doing anything dangerous. Only Geoffrey keeps saying — ' She looked up quickly at Ted, afraid that at the mention of Geoffrey's name, he would flare up. But he didn't. He looked pensive, as if for the first time he might agree with the congressman's warnings.

Cindy emerged from the building carrying a paper cup filled with water, and Susan drank thirstily.

'Thanks,' she said.

'Do you want some more?'

'No, I'll be fine. I'll come up now.'

Cindy trailed behind them as Susan said, 'I must look a mess.'

But Ted wasn't listening. 'I wonder if they — '

'Who?' Her brain was still fuzzy, but she sensed that Ted's thoughts were leading somewhere.

'Oh, nothing. You sure you're all right?'

'Yeah.'

This time when the elevator came, Cindy and Ted followed her in and stood protectively on either side of her. She felt uneasy, but she would have to get over her fears if she was ever going to work again.

She smiled tiredly as they got off on their floor. Only the suspicion that something more threatening than a blown fuse and a broken alarm bell was involved outweighed her embarrassment at being the center of attention. She shoved her hair back. 'I feel pretty dirty.'

'Why don't you go home and shower?' Cindy said.

'I think I will.' She could just go to her apartment, call Emily and let her know she was all right. Poor Emily must have had a fright getting up this morning to find her gone. Of course she might have assumed Susan had slept at the apartment last night.

Susan sat at her desk for a while, drinking

the coffee Cindy made for her. Then she called her aunt, letting Emily know she was all right. After calming Emily's fears, Susan hung up, having promised to be home this evening. Then she got up. 'Okay. I'll see you in a while,' she said to the others.

She walked down the stairs this time, telling herself she needed to stretch her legs, not that she was avoiding the elevator. Outside in the sunlight she felt better. She shook her hair out behind her, her spirits gradually lifting with each step. But when she reached her car, the sun seemed to go in. Washington had many cloudy days, but this was the darkness of a hidden menace, and she felt a knot in her stomach.

Susan drove slowly through the streets. Georgetown thronged with pedestrians even on a Monday morning. She parked in the garage and then walked around the house. As she started up the front steps, she paused to examine the vines that covered three-quarters of the brick house. Those same vines that a Peeping Tom had climbed up a few nights ago. Was he just a Peeping Tom? And what of last night's 'accident'? A chill seized her as she stepped down to the sidewalk again and approached the vines leading up to her window above. Stepping between the low shrubbery, she grabbed a handful of creepers and tried to get a foot-hold. The vines easily held her weight. Then she lowered herself before Elizabeth came out, wondering what she was doing.

Her misgivings were unanswered, unexplained. She unlocked the front door and climbed the stairs to her apartment. As she pushed her door open, it creaked heavily. The place smelled musty, uninhabited. But nothing was changed. The same books lay on the worktable. She walked through to the bedroom and sat down on the bed.

Then she lay back and stared at the ceiling. Was Geoffrey right? Did someone want to scare them off the track? If so, why? And who? Why was she being targeted? In another few days, Congress would take the matter out of their hands, anyway. But was someone trying to prevent that from happening? She was suddenly tired of pursuing and being pursued. Her lids dropped, and with her clothes on, she fell asleep.

Susan awoke as the sun was going down. She yawned and stretched her sore muscles. Already a sense of resolve was pervading her as she began to gather her thoughts. She undressed and turned the water on for a shower.

She would not give up. The AHG must be close to its target; otherwise it wouldn't be creating so much backlash. She would continue with her research. In another few days she would turn it over to Congress. But there was still work to be done, and she wasn't going to waste any time. She would go to the Library of Congress tomorrow. There were a few facts she needed to dig up.

★ ★ ★

Susan climbed the regal steps of the Library of Congress and passed through the baroque rotunda before entering the main reading room. She approached the research guidance desk. Usually she just went ahead to the card files, but she already knew she wouldn't find what she wanted there.

A thin young man with glasses looked up. 'May I help you?'

'Yes. I'm doing research on an organization's past records. They may not be in English.'

'I see,' said the young man. 'What organization?'

'Globenet.'

'What do you wish to know specifically?'

'I'd like to check the records from its founding in 1935. I've already checked the card catalog. There's nothing there.'

'Scorpio will help you.' He pointed to the

blinking computer terminal across the entry-way from where he sat. 'Our information retrieval system.'

'Oh, of course.' She had seen the computer but had never used it.

She walked to the terminal and flipped open the user manual. Following the manual, she signed into the file for information on Globenet. Then she browsed through the index for items that caught her eye. The commands were not difficult, and in two minutes she had retrieved a set of records that contained data on Globenet's history. She turned to the research guidance desk clerk.

'These documents listed in the National Archives — are copies here also?'

'For the most part, no. Many materials are deposited in the National Archives after they've been released from classification as security data. But if it is not in published form, it does not come here.'

'I see. Thank you.' She made note of the documents she would see later at the National Archives and continued to browse. She was not sure exactly what she was looking for, but she wanted to know more about the men who founded Globenet and try to put a finger on just what their original purpose had been. She had a funny feeling that the men running that organization today might have a different purpose from the one stated in all the PR about them, and she wondered how far back it might go.

Among the titles listed were reports by the Allied Control Authority; an official memorandum entitled 'Facts Concerning Globenet' and others. Also listed were *Records of the Third Reich*. Now that piqued her interest. Apparently, Nazi Germany had been a member of Globenet. This listing intimated that the Nazi Germany members had left some records. It would be interesting to see how Nazis had used the information available to them as members of Globenet during the war.

She filled out call slips for materials located in the library itself and headed for the central desk. She was conscious of energy surging through her, as it always did when she was on the trail. It was the excitement that gripped her when she was going after a problem, delving into something. Most people thought of research as boring but not Susan. To her, research meant being on the edge of a mystery, digging up information that would shed light on issues the world had overlooked. It made her feel alive.

After turning in her call slips at the central desk, she went to one of the circular reading tables to await her materials. As she waited, she surveyed the other readers — a handful of students, writers or professionals of one sort or another.

Then her roaming eyes stopped suddenly. Irwin Bradshaw sat at the front end of the circular table she occupied. He hadn't noticed her, and she instinctively shrank back. He was thumbing through a report of some sort. Susan wondered what it was.

Finally, a librarian brought her documents to her. She skimmed over much of it, but her attention was arrested by certain facts. Globenet had commenced operations in 1935 in Vienna, Austria, and in 1941 their files were moved from Vienna to a house in Berlin. They were reindexed, and operations were continued right up to the end of the war. Now, she learned, Globenet refused to use its files to track Nazi war criminals, because Globenet considered Nazi crimes to have been political. The thought stunned her. Article 4 of Globenet's constitution stated, 'It is strictly forbidden for the organization to intervene in any political, military, religious or racial matters.'

But, she noted on her yellow pad, they obviously had not understood what the Nuremberg trials had been all about — to make sure the world knew the barbarism the

Nazi regime was guilty of so that such a thing would never happen again.

But now here was Globenet, with its world network of criminal information, refusing any help to track Nazi war criminals. It made Susan wonder . . . But what could be the link to false reports? If only she could see the connection.

Drawn deeper into the shadowy world that emerged before her, she read through the afternoon until closing time. So submerged was she that the librarian from the central desk came to rouse her. He tapped her on the shoulder, making her jump.

'I'm sorry, but it's quarter to five. The materials must be returned before closing.'

'Oh,' said Susan, 'I'm sorry. Yes, I've done enough for today. I believe I'll put these on reserve.' The librarian nodded. Susan filled out the necessary slips and left for the day, wondering idly if Geoffrey would approve.

As she pulled to the edge of the parking lot and stopped to look for traffic, she noticed Irwin Bradshaw standing on the curb near the end of the block. A black limousine pulled up and a door opened on the passenger side. A large man got out and exchanged a few words with Bradshaw, who then got in. Then the other man, in an ill-fitting gray suit, walked away. She couldn't see his face clearly but noticed that he was terribly pockmarked.

* * *

When Susan returned to the library on Wednesday, she noticed that the thin young man with the glasses wasn't at the research guidance desk. Instead, a heavier-set man with dark hair sat there. She passed him by, going to get the materials she had placed on reserve.

There a surprise awaited her. The materials were gone. A girl with long black hair pulled back severely handed Susan back her call slips. 'Those materials have been checked out. They are not available.'

Susan was stunned. Who else would be reading about the early history of Globenet?

'But they were on reserve,' she said. 'Who checked them out?'

The dark-haired girl frowned. 'I wouldn't know. There's no record that they were on reserve. Are you sure you put them on reserve?'

'Of course I'm sure.' Susan felt the anger and frustration rise in her.

'If you let me have your name, I'll call you when they are returned.'

'How long will they be out?' Susan said, becoming short with the girl.

'The reader may have them all day. I don't know.'

'I can't wait all day,' Susan snapped, losing patience completely. The girl glared at Susan. Heads began to turn in their direction.

Susan lowered her voice. 'I need to have the information for a congressional subcommittee hearing. It's important.' She wrote out her name. 'Please call me when the materials have been turned in.'

The girl shrugged. 'Very well.'

'Thank you.' Susan turned to survey the reading room. About thirty people were working today. She was tempted to peer over shoulders to see who was reading her materials. She started to walk past the first few readers, but as soon as she slowed down, they looked at her strangely. No, this would never work. They had already heard her raise her voice at the desk. She would just have to wait.

She sat down at one of the reading tables. Suddenly, her eye was caught by a pock-marked man in a gray coat with a brown tie, holding a sheaf of papers. She flinched. She was sure he was the same man she had seen talking with Bradshaw yesterday. She felt her face growing hot. Was someone trying to harass her again? The thought made her angry, though, not frightened this time.

She watched the man out of the corner of her eye. Finally she caught a glimpse of the cover, and she knew he was reading 'Facts Concerning Globenet.' She stood up. But she knew she should not cause a disturbance inside the reading room. She would wait outside and accost him when he left.

She got up and walked out to the foyer. When she reached the main doors, she glanced over her shoulder. No one followed her. She emerged into sunlight. As she descended the steps, a thousand questions formed in her mind. Most important, she needed to know who the man in the library was.

She got coffee from a vendor with a truck near the sidewalk. Then she walked back up to sit at one of the wooden tables near the entrance.

After a half hour, she got tired of waiting and went back into the building. In the main reading room, her eyes adjusted to the lack of sunlight. Then she gave a start. The man reading the Globenet materials wasn't there. The seat he had occupied was empty, and the light was turned off.

Her gaze shifted to the central desk. There he was, returning his materials. She caught her breath.

He turned and came her way. As he passed

her, he glanced briefly at her, but words stuck in her throat. What could she ask him that would make any sense? It was probably just an administrative slipup and a coincidence. But she summoned her courage and followed him out.

'Excuse me,' she said, trailing him into the rotunda. 'Sir,' she said sharply enough to make him stop and turn.

'Are you speaking to me?' he asked in a nasal voice.

'Yes. I was wondering about that report you were reading. The one on Globenet?'

He looked at her but said nothing.

'I'm a graduate student,' she improvised. 'I'm researching the same subject for a class. I wonder if you could help me with something.'

'What?'

'Well — ' She panicked, unable to think of what to ask. 'Perhaps since we're both researching the same subject, we could share bibliographies.' She tried to make it sound like a simple offer, one researcher to another.

A shield came down over the man's face, and he said crisply, 'I'm sorry. I haven't the time.' And he turned and walked out.

She returned to the desk, squelching her frustration. The dark-haired girl had been replaced by the thin young man with glasses from yesterday. Susan explained that her materials had just been checked in and asked if she could have them now. Then she sat down.

In a moment, the librarian returned with some of the documents. But 'Facts Concerning Globenet' was missing. She snatched at the young man's sleeve as he was about to leave.

'There's something missing.' Then she saw the call slip sticking out of one of the other reports.

'Oh, yes,' he said. 'That one hasn't been returned.'

'But it has,' she said. 'I just saw the man return it.'

'I'm sorry,' said the librarian. 'You must be mistaken.'

Susan fumed inwardly as he walked away. She sat down to examine the materials at hand, but the pages blurred before her. Her mind kept returning to Irwin Bradshaw and to the strange man who had been here before her. He must work for Bradshaw.

Then something caught her eye. On a blank left-hand page of the Allied Control Authority report, some of the ink from the right-hand page opposite had left a faint impression. Then she looked more closely at the binding, feeling along the gutter. A page had definitely been removed, probably with a razor. She studied the faint ink on the left-hand page. It was barely noticeable, but she made out two backward S's at the right. When she had copied down the configuration backward and then turned the number around, it came out 'SS337265.' She looked across from the page that had inadvertently served as an ink blotter and found the tail end of a discussion about someone in Globenet at the time. The missing page obviously told who, but on the page remaining, the last half of the sentence on the top of the page said 'Berlin Document Center.' She jotted down the name. What was in the Berlin Document Center? The identity of the man with the SS number? She would look into it. She slipped the note with the rest of her papers into her bag. She thought again of the man with the pock-marked face. If he had clipped the page, whoever he was working for was obviously hiding something. She would have to find out what.

★ ★ ★

On Thursday morning Geoffrey finished packing his bags. Mrs. Hazlett's New Mexico counterpart, Serrita Consuelo, would look after the house and collect the mail while he was gone. He was fortunate with housekeepers — fortunate in many ways. Only since he'd met Susan did his desire to create a home life seem to put all other thoughts aside. But first he had to rescue her from the circles she was unknowingly moving in.

Riding to the airport in the back of a taxi, he stared idly at the city of Albuquerque, as it passed below the expressway, and the surrounding mountains. But already his thoughts were in Washington, and he was adding up the facts he'd read about Globenet and putting them together with the false reports the AHG had brought to the subcommittee's attention. He felt an uneasy sense of anxiety, as if he were sitting on a bomb that was about to go off and yet he couldn't stop it.

The sun was high when Geoffrey's DC-10 took off. He leaned back against the seat and stared at the papers in front of him while passengers around him watched the ground slip away beneath them. Having read glamorized accounts of Globenet and remembering the James Bond-type image of international police agents in films, he had turned to Globenet's own PR. 'An intergovernmental police force . . . Globenet's task is to hunt down and arrest international criminals . . . a law-enforcement agency made up of the police of nations around the free world . . . '

But statistics showed otherwise. Last year only eighteen percent of Globenet's investigations had led to arrests. Their files were full of petty crimes. They seemed to pass on no information about really big crimes or internationally known criminals. How was it that this world force of police let the really big fish slip through its net? It almost looked as if it were planned, and that's what Geoffrey had suspected from the beginning. They kept their computer banks busy with small fry, passing on false reports in an attempt to keep the police of the world occupied while the bigger criminals got away.

And why? Obviously someone within Globenet's structure intended it to be so. Perhaps Globenet harbored these major criminals for its own purposes.

Again Geoffrey thought of Ted Branagan's background. His information told him that Ted had been an informer while in graduate school. He was paid for criminal information he discovered among his peers — for petty crimes like possession of marijuana or information on who originated riots on campus. And his contacts had been police associated with Globenet. Of course that had been a long time ago. And he might have left the country because he had a change of heart.

If only Geoffrey were sure.

Perhaps it was all right. It was possible Ted had gone to work for the AHG because he saw that there was a potential for abuse. Or perhaps he had merely wanted to quit and his superiors had put pressure on him. But Geoffrey hated the fact that Susan worked with Ted. And she believed in him. He couldn't make her see it any other way until Ted wanted to tell her the whole story. And if Geoffrey questioned Ted directly, he would probably deny it — or accuse Geoffrey of interfering.

He rubbed his forehead with the palm of his hand. God, he wished this airplane would move faster. He desperately wanted to get back to Washington. He was worried that everything was not all right. When he had called Susan on Sunday, her aunt had said she was at work, but she hadn't answered the office phone, either. Then, when he spoke to her Monday night, she had sounded tired, though she had said nothing was wrong.

It was one thing to confront an issue in which everything was clear-cut, Geoffrey thought — when you knew who the opposition was. But who was the enemy here — someone running Globenet? But who? Its founders? Its present leaders? He thought he might try to see Globenet's secretary general and ask him a few questions.

Susan's image floated in front of his face. There was a time, he recalled, when he was like her, when he was young and idealistic and had no problem delving right into the thick of it.

But wasn't that what had attracted him to Susan? She still had the fight in her. And he didn't really want to kill it, only he was so afraid for her. She was young, committed, courageous . . . Suddenly Geoffrey felt older than his forty-two years.

* * *

Thursday morning, Susan stood on the library steps, watching Irwin Bradshaw approach. He wasn't yet looking at her, but as he took the steps, she moved in front of him. 'What is SS337265?'

He jumped, then stared angrily at her, a dark shade of red appearing in splotches over his face, his thin lips drawn in a straight line. But Susan knew she had the advantage. After a long and restless night, she had decided to confront Bradshaw or his flunky directly if either one showed up again today.

'I don't know what you mean,' he said.

But Susan held her ground. 'I believe you do,' she said. 'You were reading the same material I was. Or at least your man was yesterday. And where is the missing page?'

'I don't know what you're trying to pull, Miss Franks, but you're behaving rather oddly. What business is it of yours what I read?'

'I think you know the answer to that.'

'My dear young woman, if you mean the work the congressional subcommittee is doing, best leave it to us.'

Susan tapped her foot, gazing down at him.

'An argument will get us nowhere, you know,' he said with a lift of his thin eyebrow. 'I suggest we end this discussion and move on to more productive things.'

Susan pulled herself up. 'Very well. Then if you haven't got the materials I need on hold somewhere or if your flunkies haven't removed the relevant pages, I'll proceed to my work.'

He gave her a thin smile and gestured as if all of the Library of Congress awaited her presence. 'Good day, then,' he said.

She glared her response and waited until he went around her and continued up the steps. Then she followed him in to make sure he wasn't going to play any games with her today. If a reporter had been waiting on the steps to interview her, she could imagine her responses:

The reporter might have said, 'Miss Franks, do you have any comments on the subcommittee studying Globenet's activities?'

She would have responded with 'Irwin Bradshaw is a sneaky son of a bitch. You can bet he's going to throw a monkey wrench in the works, though we don't know just what his connection is.'

'And Geoffrey Winston?' the imaginary reporter might have asked. 'What is your relationship to him?'

'He doesn't believe a woman is equipped for investigative research.'

'Has he asked you to give it up?'

'Not in so many words, but I can feel the strain.'

'And your colleague Ted Branagan. You've known him for some time. What can you say about his devotion to the cause?'

'We used to be friends,' she said to herself, 'but people, things, have come between us. I'm no longer sure.'

Suddenly, Susan felt very lonely. Her anger was not much comfort. Her heels clicked on the marble floors, and she pushed through the swinging doors to the main reading room.

9

Geoffrey slammed the door shut on the Audi. He muttered under his breath as he crossed the lawn and took the steps two at a time. The banging of the screen door brought Emily from the kitchen and reached Susan's ears upstairs, where she was just waking up from a nap. She blinked her eyes and pushed back the cobwebs from her brain. She had only meant to nap for fifteen minutes, but when she looked at the clock, she saw she had been lying down for nearly an hour.

She heard the rising voices as Emily asked Geoffrey into the living room. Susan got up, hastily checked her appearance, ran a comb through her hair and hurried down the stairs.

Then the smile died on her lips as the thrill of seeing Geoffrey turned into sudden apprehension when she met the chilly look in his eyes. He stopped in mid-sentence, seeming to forget that Emily was there as he looked at Susan. His icy gaze warmed slightly, and an expression of longing came into his eyes.

'Geoffrey,' Susan said, the sleepiness not quite gone from her voice.

Emily said, 'Well, I'm sure you'll excuse me,' and disappeared.

Susan took two steps toward him, and then he had her in his arms. Warmth flooded through her. 'Oh, Geoffrey, you've been gone so long!'

'I was crazy with fear when they told me what had happened. Why didn't you tell me when I called?' He kissed her hair, her ears, her eyes, as she looked up inquiringly.

'They — who?' she asked, avoiding his question.

'Your colleagues. Cindy and that redhead. I stopped at the office as soon as I got in town. They told me you were here, that you'd left early after going to the library today.' He looked grim. 'Then they told me what happened Sunday. Why didn't you tell me? I'd have come back early.'

He felt her shoulders and arms as if to see that nothing was broken. Then, assuring himself that she was all in one piece, he became his commanding self again. But for a moment Susan had glimpsed a more vulnerable side of him that she always hoped lay beneath his self-assured exterior.

He straightened, exhaling a long breath of air. 'I'm starved. I hope you haven't eaten.'

'No. I'll get my bag and tell Emily we're off.'

They picked a family restaurant she had been to with her aunt. Once settled into a comfortable booth and their orders taken, they gazed a long time at each other. Susan felt as though Geoffrey had been gone a year. She blushed, embarrassed that her own emotions showed so easily, for she had no doubt that he could read her face like a book.

Geoffrey seemed to satisfy himself that he at least had her back in his keeping, and turned his thoughts to more serious matters. 'Susan, you don't know how frightened I was when I heard what had happened.'

Her heart warmed at his concern. 'I'm sorry you even had to know about it. I-I felt guilty that I'd gotten myself into a spot like that. Just careless, I guess.' She looked down. 'I was afraid you'd say I told you so.'

'I would never throw that up to you. I just can't stand being afraid someone is going to hurt you. Susan, you don't have to be involved in all this. Congress has its own investigative team. We have a budget to hire our own researchers.

'I was afraid the AHG would get in over its head. I was prepared for dealing with this when a number of my constituents complained of the same thing you were going after. But I was prepared for the danger. I knew what I was up against. I was afraid you didn't.'

She lifted her chin an inch. 'Then you want me out of it?'

He paused, the conflict evident in his eyes. 'Yes,' he finally said.

'But Geoffrey, what else would I do? I want to be a part of it. I can't help it.'

He leaned back against the booth, looking at her. 'I know that you wouldn't be happy in any other line of work.'

'That's right. It's part of me.' Her stubbornness fought against the other emotions that were churning within her. Being with Geoffrey brought her an immense sense of relief. How easy it would be to transfer the burden to him, to let him take care of her.

The food came, and she frowned at her plate, lifting her hand to push a section of dark hair back over her shoulder. 'Geoffrey, it's not that I don't appreciate your concern. Sometimes I wish that I could forget it. But I can't. I'm in too deep, like — ' She had almost said, 'Like Ted,' but stopped.

A grim look passed over Geoffrey's face. He was a grown man, authoritative and experienced in government business, but in this situation he felt helpless. He knew they were getting close to the source of the corruption, that before the next subcommittee hearing was over, more likely than not, all hell would break loose. He just did not want Susan in it. The rising warmth in his body infused his thoughts.

'Susan, will you marry me?' He paused, knowing he had to offer more of a solution than that.

She widened her eyes. 'And do what? I mean, that's not what I mean.' She swallowed. 'Of course I want to marry you. But, but — '

He stopped her. 'I don't mean you shouldn't work. I'm sure there are other — ' he paused ' — safer causes to work for.'

She eyed him uncertainly. 'Perhaps.' She studied her Reuben sandwich. 'Perhaps there is a way of compromising,' she said, though at the moment she wasn't sure what that might be. She didn't want to hide in the comfort of a man's protection. She would always want to stick her nose where it didn't belong. That was part of her character. At the very core of her being, she knew that her commitment was real. She could never give up her causes. When there was a job to be done, she wanted to roll up her sleeves and do it. But she was beginning to revise her judgment about Geoffrey's views.

She made herself confront him. 'Geoffrey,

please don't make me give up the AHG. Please don't ask me to make the choice.'

'You know I would never force you to do that,' he said quietly.

'I didn't think you would.'

'You know I want to,' he continued, 'but I can't. You have courage, Susan. A sense of justice and truth. Those things would be wasted in another job, wouldn't they?'

'Exactly. I suppose if you love me, you have to love that part of me, too. The shoe is usually on the other foot, isn't it? I mean, it's usually a woman marrying a policeman or a pilot or a sports-car driver, and it's usually the woman who spends sleepless nights worrying if her husband will come home alive the next day.' But it wasn't really very funny. 'I'm sorry,' she said, brushing her fingers against his, where his hand lay near his coffee cup. 'I know it's not the same.'

'No.' He gave her a sardonic smile. 'But you do seem to insist on playing cops and robbers.' He reached for her hand, the warmth of his touch shooting pangs of longing through her. In a hushed voice, he said, 'I just don't want your life in danger.'

They ate silently for a time. The cheese from her sandwich melted in her mouth, and the tangy sauerkraut bit into her tongue. Geoffrey turned his attention to his chili burger, and in a quarter of an hour, their stomachs sated, they signaled the waitress for more coffee.

The warm liquid soothed Susan's throat. Revived by the food, she soon felt like talking again. 'I did speak to Ted,' she told Geoffrey.

'Oh?'

She felt guilty, talking about her friend behind his back, but she plunged on. 'He told me about a number of activities he'd been involved in, but he didn't say anything about being an informer.'

Geoffrey frowned. 'Of course he might not.'

'He might have a very good reason not to.' She felt her old defenses rising. 'Oh, Geoffrey, I used to be so sure.' Then she gathered her emotions and her thoughts, trying to sound calm and rational. 'I just want to see justice done. It must be possible to catch the criminals — the real criminals, that is. Maybe that's what Ted wants to do. Maybe he had pressure put on him at one time. Maybe he just wants to see those people brought to justice.'

'I hope so,' Geoffrey said. 'For your sake.'

'Then you see why I can't quit now.'

A pensive look came over Geoffrey's face. 'Yes, I do. I may not like it, but I do understand.' He was powerless to argue her out of it. She had twisted herself around his heart, and at that moment he felt an even stronger need for her.

They finished eating, then went out to his car. As he opened the door for her, he touched her briefly. She paused before getting in and leaned slightly against him. He kissed her temple, his hand sliding around her waist. But then he gently guided her into the car. He had been away from her a long time, and her very nearness aroused him to a point that was nearly unbearable. He wanted to have her alone with him.

Neither spoke as Geoffrey followed the roads into the city. With unspoken agreement, they drove to his apartment, and when he glanced at her, she seemed to be satisfied with watching out the window.

He felt the blood surge through his veins as he drove. Ancient instincts were overriding all rational thought. He wanted to protect Susan from the evil forces he knew she was up against, but she refused to play the role of a lady needing rescuing. He wished she would rely on him a little more. He parked the Audi in the garage under his building; then they rode up in the elevator to his apartment. At his door she stood near him, and he could sense that she wanted the same thing he did.

The apartment was as neat as a pin, thanks

to Mrs. Hennessy. He closed the door behind Susan, then followed her into the living room. Then she was in his arms, and he held her close, drinking in her presence, her intoxicating odor. His blood throbbed as he began to kiss her, and she moved willingly in his arms. Thought fled for both of them.

'Susan,' he whispered, his hands moving of their own accord over her. She moaned hungrily, and her arms went around him as he kissed her deeply. She moved against him, exciting him beyond all reason. Then he guided her into the bedroom, and without speaking, they shed jackets, belts, shoes. He took off his shirt. Then he turned to find her fumbling with the buttons on her blouse. He kissed her again as he finished unbuttoning it. Then he slid his hands inside her blouse and pulled her to him again.

He uttered a moan as he touched her tender breasts, gazing down at the soft, voluptuous whiteness before him. All of a sudden he could wait no longer. They shed the rest of their clothing, and she slid into the bed. He followed her, his hands roaming her smooth skin, his mouth seeking her taut nipples. He ran his hands down the curve of her waist and hip. Then his mouth found hers as he touched her downy softness with his fingers, and he uttered a moan as her hands wrapped around him, caressing, rubbing. Half berating himself for acting so quickly, he was on top of her, but she opened herself eagerly to him, and then they were moving together, thrilling as every inch of his skin touched hers. He wanted to be completely a part of her in every way.

The sharp yearning was centered in the lower part of their bodies as his need built quickly, but he held back as long as he could before his own powerful surge burst forth. She arched against him, every muscle of hers accommodating him. Then slowly they descended together, holding each other tightly, afraid to let go as the darkness closed around them.

★ ★ ★

Gradually morning stole through the drapes. As light moved toward her, Susan stirred, pushing the bedcovers from her. She stood, naked, looking at the earth-toned wallpaper around her. Then she walked to the bathroom and turned on the shower.

She stepped into the comforting warm water and closed her eyes. How she wished it would wash away her problems. She lost count of the minutes, letting the water run over her. Then she shampooed her hair.

After the steamy shower, she toweled her hair and slipped into a blue terry-cloth robe she found on a hook on the bathroom door. It was large and draped her body nearly to her ankles. She cuddled into it, breathing in the fresh laundered scent.

She walked softly through the bedroom and down the hall as the smell of bacon and coffee drifted her way. Geoffrey was at the stove.

'Hi,' she said, coming up to him and weaving her arms around his waist. He turned in her grasp, reached inside the robe and cupped her breast as he gave her a good-morning kiss.

'Hungry?' he asked, kissing her between each word. 'Toast . . . jam . . . eggs . . . coffee?'

She pushed him away playfully. 'Just like mother's cooking.'

'I don't know,' he said, returning to the frying bacon. 'I've never been a mother, just a father.'

She laughed. 'When are those sons of yours coming for a visit?'

'Next month, as a matter of fact.' He put down the fork and reached out to pull her next to his side. 'I want you to meet them.'

She snuggled under his arm. 'I want to.' Then she disentangled herself and began setting the table. They served themselves breakfast and sipped hot coffee as the morning sun bathed the dining area in its warmth. 'Heavenly,' she breathed. Such a contrast to the issues facing them both.

She reshuffled her thoughts, then said, 'Perhaps there is a way of compromising.'

'Oh?'

She wasn't really sure what that compromise would be, but she wanted to make the effort to find it. 'You know, Geoffrey, we ought to put some of our information together. Perhaps we each have different pieces to the puzzle. If we just piece them together, we might see the whole picture.'

He nodded. 'I thought of that while I was out West.' Then he frowned. 'We've each combed over a lot, but perhaps we've missed something.'

She leaned forward, the excitement already building. 'I suppose it will all come out in the hearing, but — '

'We need to know before that.'

She said solemnly, 'Yes. It's even possible that we can figure out who is trying to foil our plans.'

He lowered his lids slightly. 'Yes.'

She twisted the belt of the robe in her hands. 'It's just frustrating — '

'What?'

'That we have to play fair — '

'When they don't,' he finished for her.

She nodded. They were in accord at last. The adrenaline flowed through her veins. 'Geoffrey, we can work together now.'

'Yes. We've been opposing each other for too long.'

'And for all the wrong reasons,' she said.

They finished dressing, and in half an hour, the dishes cleared, they were again seated at the dining table. Susan had out a pad and pen. It sometimes helped her to diagram the facts she had at hand, to draw connecting lines, to see the relationships more easily.

She told Geoffrey she had found out that Globenet operated during the war. She told him also about seeing Irwin Bradshaw and the other man at the library and about the missing page in the report. She described the imprint of the SS number she had deciphered. She had inquired about it at the Berlin Document Center by telephone yesterday, and they had solved the riddle for her.

'Obviously either Bradshaw or the man who worked for him sliced away the page, but they didn't go far enough. It was Viktor Bruning's SS number, the Berlin Document Center told me, and they're sending me a photo to prove it.'

'And Viktor Bruning was president of Globenet as late as 1972,' Geoffrey said.

'So we know the Nazis had control of Globenet at one point.'

'Yes, and the same files are used today.'

'They don't even deny it.'

Geoffrey rose, paced around the living room, massaging the back of his neck with his hand. He said, 'I begin to see a pattern. All points bulletins are put out by Globenet frequently. They concentrate on small-time operators, a lot of young Americans accused of petty crimes. This is just speculation, but suppose the men controlling Globenet still have Nazi interests.'

A shudder of apprehension ran down Susan's spine at the thought. Some of the old Nazis were still alive. But to think that they had control of an organization as big and as all-encompassing as Globenet was chilling.

'What could be their purpose?' she asked, almost afraid of the question. 'Most of the old Nazis are dead.'

Geoffrey came to a stop in front of her. 'Yes, but more than thirty thousand Nazis were unaccounted for at the end of the war. And the older men may have trained other, younger men to replace them. If Globenet circulates false reports about suspects, intentionally confuses issues, they keep the police of the world occupied while they use Globenet's operation to cover up their own actions.'

'Which are?'

'We don't know that, do we? Smuggling? Drug trafficking? Whatever it is, it's got to be profitable for them.'

'Yes,' she said slowly. 'And what would they be wanting the profits for?'

'If they're Old-World Nazis, a number of things. To protect themselves, preventing their extradition to countries that have indictments out on them. To finance their careers, to keep them away from the Nazi hunters who still seek to bring them to justice. Or — ' he paused as the horror of the idea sunk in ' — to finance the neo-Nazi groups creeping up on this country today. The SS was a mystique, a religion of race and blood, in addition to being Hitler's private arm. And there are men no one knows about dedicated to similar causes today. Men who believe in the insane dreams originated in a war lost.'

Susan was still as the weight of the words sank in. 'The world must have been mad,' she said, thinking of Hitler's regime.

'It was mad,' he said. He continued, a biting edge to his voice. 'And there are those who would do that sort of thing again. They are the ones who seek dominance through a global police state. Globenet refuses to use its files to track Nazi war criminals because Globenet considers Nazi crimes to have been political. These people are serious about controlling world politics for their own benefit. Through Globenet they have access to the largest data base in criminal dossiers. And by cleverly linking the police forces of the world, Globenet has put itself into a unique position. It makes no arrests, but it passes information between cooperating countries and circulates false reports on its enemies, even though they may be innocent.'

Susan shivered. When innocent citizens first came to the AHG complaining of false reports circulating against them, she never would have guessed the trail would lead to Globenet. And that in the higher echelons of that organization there might be men controlling the police of the world in an effort to live out their lives away from the justice that awaited them if they made their true identities known.

'But Geoffrey,' she said, sketching lines on the paper in front of her to help her fight off the dizziness that had threatened, 'they aren't really invincible — only if they remain unknown. If we expose them, there is nothing left for them to stand on.'

'But first we must know who they are.'

'Yes, but there must be a link. Someone connected to them. We just have to find the link. The person — ' She stopped as a sudden thought came into her mind. 'The person who is protecting Globenet's interests.'

She looked up. Geoffrey was looking out the window, far away in thought. 'Yes,' he said. 'It would be a person in a position to protect their interests.'

She turned her head toward the window, following his gaze. 'Then if someone is harassing us . . . ' The horror of it seized her, and for a moment she felt sorry for Geoffrey. This was what he had to face every day, the fear that she might indeed be swept away from him. She struggled with the thoughts, then forced them from her. Now was not the time for weakness. Now was a time to act. 'So what, or whom, are we fighting?' she asked.

Geoffrey shifted his weight away from the window. 'We are fighting the threat of an elite group of men bent on world domination for their own benefit.'

'It's an ancient theme, isn't it?' she said in a low voice.

'Unfortunately, yes. Evil's been around for a long time.'

★ ★ ★

243

Ted leaned on Susan's desk and spoke softly. Susan strained to listen, surprised at his tone, for his booming voice could usually be heard down the hallway when he was addressing someone. But now she realized his words were meant only for her.

'I have a surprise for you.'

'For me?'

'For us, really.'

'Oh?'

'I am collecting on a favor,' he said with a knowing look. She looked at him quizzically.

'A friend at the Department of Treasury has invited me to pay him a visit.'

She sat up straight. 'Oh?'

'He's an inspector for the IRS. He has access to the TECS computer.'

At first she did not understand Ted's inference, but when it dawned on her what he was suggesting, she paled. 'You're not going to — '

But he said, 'Exactly. I'm going to take a look. Want to come along?'

'Ted, you aren't. We have no right — '

'Why not?'

Her own words came back to her. She had told Geoffrey they would never do anything illegal, that they were certain they could bring facts to light by using the law, not by circumventing it.

'Susan, we've got to take a look. It might give us a clue as to where the majority of these false reports originate. We ought to be able to see if Globenet is in fact the originator.'

'But even if we do find something out, we can't use it as evidence. We can't testify to a congressional subcommittee that we broke into the Treasury Department and used the TECS computer illegally.' The thought was appalling. 'Ted, what you suggest is the very kind of criminal action the AHG is trying to stop.'

'Oh, come off it, Susan. You know we're not criminals.'

'I know that, but it doesn't make any difference.'

'It most certainly does. It's the intention that makes it right. We're on the side of justice.'

She stared at him in stupefaction, last night's conversation echoing in her brain. 'It's not fair that we have to play fair,' she had said. 'When they don't,' Geoffrey had finished. Now here was Ted standing before her, suggesting that they tarnish what she considered their saintly reputation. She swallowed as Ted continued. 'I can see by the look in your eye what you think,' he said. 'I knew this would happen.'

'What would happen?'

'You've been seeing too much of Geoffrey Winston.'

'Oh, Ted, not that again.'

'Don't tell me he hasn't suggested you quit your activities.'

Her eyes flickered, and she knew she had given away the fact that he had guessed correctly. 'We discussed it, but we came to an understanding. I told him I would never quit.'

'Did you, now?'

'Yes, I did.'

'Well, if you're still with us, why don't you come along and help me find out what's to be learned from the computer?'

She felt compromised, trapped. How could she face Geoffrey if she compromised her integrity by participating in an illicit act herself in an attempt to foil their enemies before being foiled themselves? She looked up at Ted and saw the challenge, as if he had thrown a gauntlet at her feet. She knew she had no choice. She needed to know what Ted was going to do, disappointed as she was in his method. It seemed that his actions were exposing more and more the motivations Geoffrey suspected him of. She would have to go, if only to keep an eye on Ted. She sincerely hoped she would be able to justify her actions later.

'All right,' she said. 'I'll go.'

He stood up straight, satisfaction in his eyes. 'Good.'

10

It was nearly midnight when Susan and Ted hurried around the giant IRS complex that covered nearly a whole block between Pennsylvania and Constitution avenues. They stopped at the security guard's booth, where a uniformed guard stepped out.

'Ted Branagan,' Ted said in his most authoritative tone as he held out a pass that had been made out to him. 'We're here to see Walt Johnson, IRS Inspection Service.'

'Hold on, please,' the guard said. He stepped back into his booth and picked up a telephone. 'A Mr. Branagan and a Miss Franks to see you, sir.'

He hung up and came out of the booth. He let them through a pair of locked doors. Inside, a tall black guard rose from his desk.

'Take them to room 628,' the first man said to the second, handing him the pass.

The black guard nodded, and Ted and Susan followed him down a long corridor to the elevator. No one spoke as they rode up to the sixth floor. The guard led them past several doors and finally knocked on one near the end of the hall.

'Come in,' came a deep voice with a Texas drawl. As the guard swung the door in, a tall blond man rose from behind his desk. He had a muscular build and a face etched with lines. 'Thank you, Rudy,' he said to the guard, who nodded and shut the door behind them.

'Well, well,' said Johnson, shaking Ted's hand and smiling at Susan.

'This is my colleague, Susan Franks,' said Ted.

'Nice to meet you.' She was certain her nervousness showed as she shook hands with the IRS inspector.

Ted had met Walt Johnson several years ago in Colorado, but it had taken years of friendship for the two men to feel close enough to exchange favors of this magnitude. Johnson understood Ted, and he believed in what Ted was doing.

'Can we talk?' Ted gestured around the room, indicating that it might be bugged.

'You're as safe as you can be in Washington,' said Johnson. He pointed to countersurveillance devices attached to both phones and placed near the doors.

'Impressive,' said Ted.

'All ready? We'd better go in. In an hour the computer will be shut down for maintenance.'

A few minutes later they were in a different

wing of the sprawling building, standing in front of a glass partition. Signs indicated the temperature control, security data and the fact that the equipment inside was government property. There were burglar-alarm warnings, as well.

Johnson pulled out a platinum pass card that could be read electronically, admitting him to the computer room. He stood in the aim of a camera mounted above the door.

'When the red light goes out, move through there fast,' Johnson said, indicating the glass door. 'You have about one second after the camera takes my picture, while the film is advancing. After that it returns to the closed-circuit television system for the guard downstairs.'

Johnson inserted the card. A buzzer sounded, releasing the lock on the door. The red light by the camera went out, the glass door opened, and Ted dashed through, holding the door for Susan. Johnson followed at a more leisurely pace. The door slid shut behind him.

In the center of the brightly lit room was a large piece of computer hardware. Around the room at various work stations, stand-alone terminals, their screens blank, waited for operators. Telex machines stood silent, ready to print data sent over the network. The lowered temperature of the room made Susan shiver.

Ted stepped out into the middle of the room. 'So this is TECS,' he said.

'The Treasury Enforcement Communications System,' Johnson said, 'built in 1970. It's been operated around the clock since then.'

'And everyone's in it,' said Ted thoughtfully.

Susan's nervousness abated somewhat as she realized with some curiosity that at last she was standing in the same room with TECS impressive circuitry, which was linked to criminal justice agencies in all fifty states.

'And we're free to look?' Ted said.

'Management controls are very loose,' Johnson said. 'There's nothing concerning anyone that I'm effectively forbidden to look for on this computer. We can lay a finger on anyone at any time. If it's there, we'll find it. The data banks contain extensive dossiers on individual citizens.'

'To us everyone is a criminal,' Ted said, quoting Globenet's Secretary General Louis LeBlanc. Susan remembered her discussion with Ted about the French view of a person's guilt until he proved his innocence.

'TECS is the main storage terminal for

intelligence information on individuals, businesses, vehicles, aircraft, vessels suspected of smuggling — you name it,' Johnson said.

'The way I understand it, Globenet's investigative requests, all points bulletins and Wanted circulars are entered into TECS, and instantaneously transmitted between the U.S. office, the headquarters in France and other member countries.'

'That's right,' said Johnson. 'Teletype contact can be made with virtually all local or state law-enforcement agencies through the National Law-Enforcement Telecommunication System.'

'In other words, it's a hookup.'

'Yes.'

'And through these systems, Globenet places nationwide lookouts,' Ted said, then looking at Susan, 'TECS is the key.'

In spite of her doubts about being here, Susan was impressed by how far TECS's tentacles spread. Ted's excitement was catching. She was becoming curious herself.

'Well, let's see some suspects,' Ted suggested.

'Okay,' said Johnson. He walked to one of the small terminals and took a seat. He switched it on and quickly entered the correct commands to locate an index of dossiers on suspected criminals. Ted and Susan watched as the names rolled past on the video screen.

Susan drew in her breath. There was the name of one of the people who had come to them. A deputy sheriff in Kansas, he, along with several family members, had been listed for minor suspicion because a neighbor complained that the kids were having a noisy party.

There were also arrest records showing that the person indicted was later proved completely innocent, as Susan well knew. 'Can we tell where these reports originated?' she asked. 'I mean, who entered them?'

'Yes. See here at the end. This code shows who added data last and when. This IN is Globenet's code.'

'Then this record — ' Susan pointed to the greenish letters on the screen ' — came from Globenet itself?'

'At least this shows that someone in Globenet either entered it originally or added to it.'

He called up several more reports.

'There are a lot with that code,' she said.

'Exactly,' said Ted. 'It proves what we thought. Globenet's got their fingers in the pie.'

'Proof, but we can't use it,' said Susan, remembering they were here illegitimately.

'But at least we know.'

Susan frowned. They had other means of knowing — legal ones, even though they took longer.

Johnson pushed more keys. There was much unevaluated information concerning millions of citizens innocent of any crime at all. The more they saw, the more it was confirmed that these dossiers were indeed cluttered with uninspected data that could possibly be used to abuse private citizens who were guilty of no crime. Such a vast accumulation of speculative personal information could easily be misused.

'It's chilling,' she whispered. Susan thought she had been prepared for what she would see, but she was truly appalled. Every request for information about a suspect was entered, whether or not the person was later convicted. But she forced herself to continue to look, now that she was here. She glanced at the side of Ted's intent face.

'False reports,' she muttered.

'That's right,' he said. 'They have a grain of truth, but they're cleverly manufactured and circulated through the computer to harass certain individuals.'

'But why?'

He shook his head. 'Those in power have their reasons, that much we know. But what we see here is stretched, twisted and interpreted beyond recognition of what was probably the truth.' She could see his jaw tense as he said, 'Collecting information is a dangerous game in a world where information means power.'

'I wonder,' said Susan, feeling depressed suddenly, 'if it's even possible to straighten this out.'

'Don't ask me,' said Johnson. 'You crusaders, that's your job, isn't it?'

'Unfortunately,' said Ted.

'Now,' said Johnson, 'did you want to find out something specific?'

'Let's see if we're in it,' Susan suggested, but Ted said sharply, 'Why?' She looked up quickly at his reaction, but it made her more determined to follow her notion.

'Type in,' she said, still watching Ted. 'Type in — ' she paused again ' — my name,' she continued. 'Franks, first name Susan.'

Johnson typed her name and some codes into the computer. In a few seconds a message appeared on the screen: NEED TO KNOW.

'What's that mean?' asked Susan.

'It means the computer won't give me the information until I tell it why I need to know. Then the computer will decide whether to let me see classified information.'

A menu appeared on the screen, asking

several questions. Johnson typed in his name, ID number, date of his last request from the computer and his agency. A few seconds passed, then a short dossier appeared. They read with interest.

'Susan Franks. Graduated Arizona State University 1979. Major: history. Employed Library of Congress, Copyright Office 1981–85. Library of Science degree 1985. Joined Association for Honesty in Government 1985. Investigative work on controversial subjects. cf. Ted Branagan. Arrests: none. Violations: none.'

Susan was astonished at the detail. 'But why am I in this thing?'

'Obviously someone is interested in you,' said Johnson.

'But the data's twisted,' said Susan. 'I do research, not investigation.'

'It's the same thing to whoever entered this report,' said Johnson. 'Want to check your name, Ted? That cross-reference there is very interesting.'

Ted stiffened. 'Go ahead,' he said.

Johnson typed in the commands, then a message appeared. NO SUCH FILE.

'Hmm,' said the IRS agent. 'Nothing there.'

Susan watched Ted's carefully controlled expression. 'Are you sure?' she asked.

'I'll try again,' said Johnson. He repeated the commands. Still, the same message appeared. He shrugged. 'That's odd.'

No one said anything, and Susan was seized with the thought that there might be a reason Ted wasn't in the computer, and she was alarmed at the direction her mind was taking. Geoffrey's warnings came back full force, and she felt waves of fear come over her. Her jaw went rigid as she confronted the thought. If Ted worked with Globenet himself, that could be the reason his name wouldn't be in the computer. Nausea threatened, and she leaned on the back of a chair for support.

'Who else?' asked Johnson.

'Geoffrey Winston,' said Ted, and Susan drew in a breath.

Congressman Winston's dossier appeared on the screen, and they read for a few minutes. To Susan's relief it was mostly data she already knew: the bills he had introduced, the committees he had served on, his record as a representative in New Mexico, his education. There was one thing she didn't know. He had done some army intelligence work in Southeast Asia.

A flush crept up Susan's neck. She felt as if she were spying on people and didn't like the feeling. Still, here was proof of the reality.

Various intelligence and law-enforcement agencies entered these files into the massive computer data banks, and the data could very easily be interpreted and twisted for whatever purpose. It nauseated her that it was so incredibly time-consuming and expensive for a private citizen to get hold of his own records and straighten them out. Perhaps Ted had been right to persuade her to come. All they were doing was looking.

They spent a few more minutes looking at the records of people who had come to them with abuses, verifying what their clients had said. Then Johnson glanced at his watch. 'That about it?' he asked.

'We've seen what we came for,' said Ted.

Johnson shut down the terminal. They left the TECS area and made their way along the corridors back to Johnson's office. They talked for a few minutes, but Susan's imagination was racing on by itself. She was suddenly afraid that Ted might have been lying all this time. Her throat was dry, and her skin turned to gooseflesh. It took every ounce of control to appear calm, to shake hands with Walt. He walked them down to the guard at the desk. The black man watched them intently as they left the building and walked up the block.

Susan returned to her aunt's house, shaken by what she had seen. She wished she could just continue driving along the dark highway flanked by tall pines, not stopping until daylight rose on some peaceful peninsula somewhere where she could rest at a private cottage with the warm sun pouring in at the window.

Taking a deep breath to get a better grip on herself, she made a conscious effort to still her thoughts. She was endangering her driving by allowing her emotions to overcome her. She was tired, after all, and events were apt to take on exaggerated proportions in her mind. She evened her breathing and concentrated on the road. A pair of headlights came toward her, and she tightened her pressure slightly on the wheel, as she always did when there were other cars on the road with her.

With relief, she turned off the main road to the residential streets. A car she had noticed some distance behind her turned in, as well.

Stop it, she told herself. She really was becoming paranoid now. She turned into her aunt's street, watching in the rearview mirror to see if the other car followed her.

It did not. She let out a breath she didn't realize she'd been holding. She had told

Emily not to wait up and hoped she wouldn't disturb her aunt by coming in so late. She eased the car in next to the curb, and when she got out, she closed the door as quietly as possible. Then she inhaled a breath of night air. There was just the faintest perception of light in the sky from a half moon. Night was hastening on. How she wished it would take with it the fears and unsettled feelings she had accumulated.

She slumped her shoulders and stared at the sleeping houses around the cul-de-sac. The longing she had felt for a quiet life returned, but with it anger and frustration that the two men she was closest to in the world had brought her to this.

She turned her face up to the night sky. No, it wasn't right to blame someone else for her own condition. She was responsible for the things she had gotten into.

She sighed. Her muscles ached, and her bones felt stiff. She was tired. But it wasn't fatigue from being up most of the night. She had done that countless times before. It was fatigue from having done something she had told herself she would never do. She had crossed the line. They had crossed the line. How could the AHG stand for truth when they had cheated?

Of course Ted had said they couldn't use

the evidence in any way publicly; it had simply given them direction. They could duel more equally. Still, the bile rose in her throat. Perhaps she wasn't cut out for this kind of work, after all. She was too naive. Perhaps Geoffrey was right. It was ludicrous to think they could take on the whole government by themselves. Perhaps no one could.

Her head fell forward, and she realized she was nearly asleep on her feet. So tired. She climbed the stairs and inched open the storm door. She would think about it tomorrow.

★ ★ ★

Ted had told her not to report to work until noon. Cindy and Michael could handle the phones. But when she saw that the face of the clock on the night-stand said 10:00 A.M., she threw back the covers. In spite of the throbbing at her temples that told her she craved more rest, she fought back. They must make corrections on the statements they would be handing out at the hearing and see that copies got made today.

The phone rang; then its silence after one ring told Susan that Emily had picked it up. In a few moments her footsteps on the stairs alerted Susan. Emily tapped on the door.

'Yes, Emily, I'm wake.'

'For you, dear. Congressman Winston.'

Her heart thudded suddenly, and a clammy feeling on her skin made her want to withdraw back into the covers and ignore the call. The sickening taste of guilt rose in her throat.

'All right. I'll come down.'

'Take it in my bedroom if you want to.'

'Okay. Thanks.'

She wrapped a robe around her and made her way across the carpeted hallway, sniffing the smell of violets as she entered her aunt's bedroom. The phone sat on the corner of the nightstand, a powder-blue menace to Susan's uncomfortable mood.

'Hello.'

'Susan, are you all right?' Geoffrey's voice was filled with concern.

'Yes. I just worked late, so I took the morning off.'

A pause. She could almost see him frowning into space. 'Are you going to work later?'

'Yes. I — we have to get the statement ready for copying today.'

'Very well. When will you be finished for the day?'

'Oh, I don't know. Six, seven; it depends.'

'Finish by seven and I'll pick you up for

dinner.' It was not an invitation; it was a statement.

'Well, I suppose — '

'I'll be in front of your building — unless you'd prefer I come up.'

'No, no — I'll be there.'

'Good.' Then, in a less didactic tone, he said, 'Good-bye, Susan, and be careful today.' He hung up.

Be careful. Always be careful. She glared at the phone. Then she sighed and ran her fingers through her hair, giving her scalp a quick massage.

Her nerves were taut. She was likely to lash out at anyone who crossed her today. But she would have to get a hold on her temper, at least until she got to the office. She laughed to herself grimly. Then she could take it out on Ted. He had a few things coming.

She dressed hastily and went downstairs. If there was anything in the refrigerator, she would make some lunch. But Emily had anticipated her. Susan could smell the coffee even before she got to the kitchen. Emily had a large bowl of freshly mixed tuna fish and was slicing cucumbers at the counter.

Susan groaned when she walked into the kitchen. 'Food,' she said. 'Emily, you're perfect.'

'I thought you'd want a bite.'

'Bless you,' Susan said.

'My pleasure. I've got to eat, too, you know. Might as well make it healthy and attractive.'

Susan scooped out a generous helping of tuna on a piece of whole wheat bread, poured a fresh cup of coffee and took her plate to the table. The sun bathed the room in warmth, and some of the goblins from the night before left her. A glimmer of a thought teased the corners of her mind. It might be possible to put things to rights, even though she knew she had no basis for thinking that. She had antagonized her friend and colleague, become disappointed in what she thought were his sterling qualities; she had disappointed herself, taking part in an activity that, though justifiable from certain points of view, violated her own personal code of integrity. And she had been shaken by a man who professed to love her but who challenged her purpose and her career. A man who, though not asking her to give it up, would change her life if she let him.

How, then, did she propose to right these things? She didn't have so much a formed idea, but a sense of hope. As she watched Emily bustle around the roomy kitchen, Susan drew on the feelings of peace and security here, so different from the dark work of intrigue she was getting closer to.

Could it be possible to have both? To repair her integrity, understand those close to her, somehow find the razor's edge that was her own path in all this? Could she learn to challenge injustice while keeping her own nose clean and still be able to make a difference to the world?

She had to do it. Firm resolve began to take the place of self-doubt and questioning. She relaxed over her coffee, letting the warmth from the cup permeate her hands, the steam drift up to her face. She decided to let herself be nourished by the comfort that was offered here. Then she would gather strength and get on with it.

★ ★ ★

Geoffrey sat across from Susan at his dining-room table. From outside came a dim glow of moonlight and streetlights. He had instructed Mrs. Hennessy to cook for two, and after he had picked Susan up at work, they drove to his apartment.

Susan had tried to give him a smile, but she knew the kiss that she had given him was lacking. She was thankful that the darkness inside the car helped shield her fears. Unspoken between them was the fact that the day after tomorrow was a new hearing on findings resulting from a preliminary congressional investigation of Globenet. And underlying Susan's attempt to remain pleasant company were the reminders of Geoffrey's behavior at the last hearing.

He eyed her quizzically. 'You're awfully quiet.'

'Why, what do you mean?' She could not stop the tremor in her heart and the discomfort of his penetrating gaze. She had come so close to telling him. Could he guess? No, probably not. Even Geoffrey would probably find it hard to believe that she had spent the wee hours before dawn reading dossiers on the TECS computer at the Department of the Treasury.

She didn't dare tell him. He could accuse her in public tomorrow, and that would discredit the AHG's reputation and seriously cast doubt on their testimony.

She tried to smile at him, but she was coming more and more to realize that she was in an impossible situation when it came to Geoffrey. She could not involve herself in activities that had to be kept confidential and at the same time have a completely open and honest relationship with Geoffrey. And, she realized, looking at his face as he sipped from a crystal goblet of wine, if she were to commit herself to a relationship with him, that would be what she wanted. She would not want to have to hold anything back.

As if guessing her thoughts, Geoffrey reached across the table and touched her chin with his finger, his thumb brushing her cheek. 'Are you worried about the hearing tomorrow?'

She moved against his fingers slightly. 'Yes, of course.'

'You shouldn't be.'

'Why?'

He looked at her a long time. 'Susan, does it really matter so much to you?'

'Of course it matters.'

The tremor in her heart accelerated as his thumb continued to caress her cheek. Then he stood, carrying his wineglass to the coffee table in front of the sofa, and held out his hand for her to join him.

She rose as if under his spell. She hated the way she was drawn to him, hated the way Ted Branagan had placed seeds of doubt in her mind about him and vice versa, hated the way Geoffrey tempted her to give up her crusading. Was he on the side of the devil, there only to lure her away from her pursuit of the truth? But how could he be? He was here with her now, touching her tenderly as his mouth claimed hers. She could feel his heart beat in time with hers. Surely they believed in the same things. Surely he was a refuge, not a threat . . .

A fleeting image of Ted's face was projected into her mind. 'To us everyone is a criminal,' Ted was saying. But those weren't his words. They were the words of someone in the hierarchy of Globenet. That would be taken care of tomorrow. Tonight the evening was hers and Geoffrey's, and no one could steal it from them.

She lost herself in him as her frustrations and desire poured themselves out in a sensual exploration. Geoffrey responded with eagerness, sensing her desire to please and be pleased.

Issues were still unresolved. But let tomorrow come and the love they felt be a guiding light in their responses to each other. Finally, he pulled her gently from him and stood.

'Come,' he said softly, his arm around her shoulders as he guided her to his bedroom. Then he gently loved her, and she asked for more and more from him.

As Susan fell asleep against Geoffrey's firm back, the sheets caressing the skin he had so recently touched, a sense of peace stole over her — peace and the desire to remain beside him forever. But would the intimacy and sharing of the evening last into the light of day? When she faced him the day after tomorrow across the subcommittee chambers, would her heart still flutter? Would he look at her lovingly? Or would he challenge and cross-examine her, making her prove her worth? Only the day would show them that.

They seemed to lead a double life: one caring, intimate, creating a private world with a secret language and lovers' caresses; the other a matter of public record, every statement a matter for debate.

11

Susan opened her eyes to darkness. It took her a moment to adjust to the fact that she was alone again in her aunt's house. Immediately, she warmed at the memory of yesterday morning. She had awakened beside Geoffrey. It had been warm and delicious until the drowsiness of early morning had fled and thoughts of the day's work came into her mind. Still, she had enjoyed the moments of making coffee and listening to Geoffrey whistle as he stepped into the shower.

He had dropped her off at work, where she'd left her car the night before, and she'd walked in to be greeted by the glaring face of Ted Branagan. Cindy had ducked her head quickly to avoid the confrontation she could see was about to take place.

Instead of his usual accusations, however, Ted merely looked at Susan with the expression of a pained animal. She wanted to ignore his look, but something moved her to speak.

'I know what you're thinking, Ted.'

'Oh, I don't know how you could.'

'You're going to tell me I'm jeopardizing

our position. That I've been seen in public with Geoffrey Winston before the hearing.'

'I won't say that, Susan. All I will say is that if anything does happen to jeopardize our position as a result of your, er, ah, association with him, it won't be my fault.'

'Of course not, but Ted, I'm sure everything will go all right.' She knew it was a hopeless argument. She was powerless to persuade Ted that this time she thought Geoffrey would be a help to them.

'The hearing isn't until tomorrow. A lot could happen,' he said.

She didn't see what events could take place today that would affect tomorrow's hearing. 'WITNESS SLEEPS WITH SUB-COMMITTEE MEMBER TO BRING DOWN GLOBENET HEADS.' No, it was an unlikely headline. They were ready to testify. And they were certain that Congress's investigations would turn up additional evidence of corruption within the workings of Globenet. That organization's days were numbered.

She felt her temples begin to throb. 'Ted, let's drop it, shall we?'

After work, she had returned to Emily's and spent a quiet evening. Now she rose and turned on the lamp beside the bed. Looking out the window opposite the bed, she realized why it was so dark. A heavy mass of clouds was keeping the sun from shining. She could hear the rain splatter against the windows and see the smears where drops had splashed against the glass.

She came fully awake and began to prepare herself for the hearing. She shut off the alarm, which hadn't yet rung, and went to the bathroom to wash her face. In a few minutes, she was reaching into the closet for the tailored suit and silk blouse with wide cuffs and collar she had planned to wear. She focused on getting dressed, her mind keeping the thoughts and conflicts of the last few weeks at bay.

She could hear Emily moving about downstairs, and as she was just pulling her slip over her head, Emily knocked on the door.

'Come in,' said Susan as the slip fell into place over her body.

'I thought you'd like a cup of hot coffee while you're getting dressed.'

'Oh, my goodness. How thoughtful.' Emily knew about the hearing and probably realized Susan would dawdle over her makeup and hair today, whereas she usually just threw a sweater over her head, jumped into a pair of slacks and raced off to work.

Emily set the small tray down on the

corner of the dresser, leaving room for Susan to work on her appearance.

'How heavenly. Oh, Emily, you spoil me.'

The other woman gave her a smile. 'Like I said the other day, it's kind of nice to have someone to spoil.'

Susan felt a lump in her throat as she smiled back at her aunt. 'You know, Emily, I've enjoyed living here. I almost hate to go back to my own apartment.'

'You don't have to, you know.'

'I know,' Susan said, turning to brush her hair while still holding Emily's eyes in the mirror. 'But I can't hide out here forever.'

'Well, I don't see why not. With your parents living so far away, I rather feel like I should look out for you. Of course you're too old for that. But it's nice to have someone to do things for.'

'I know, Em. And you've been a dear.' She paused, then said, 'Emily, what do you think of Geoffrey Winston?'

A blush came into Emily's cheeks as she said, 'My goodness, he is quite a man, isn't he?'

Susan laughed. 'Well, I guess that answers that.'

Emily became more serious. 'If you really want to know what I think — I think he's the kind of man a woman could rely on. I

273

wouldn't mind someone like that coming into my life again.'

'Oh, Em, I know what you mean.' But Susan was not like her aunt in that sense. Emily had been a working woman, but not out of choice. She seemed to enjoy making a home more than she wanted a career, and she hadn't really wanted to be independent.

Susan looked at her own reflection in the mirror, but she spoke to Emily, who stood behind her. 'That's what confuses me. He is what you say he is. But I'm not sure that's what I want. He would not want me to continue with my work at the AHG.'

'Has he said as much?'

'In a way. He's said time and again the AHG has bitten off more than it can chew. But don't you see? We stick our nose into government business to prove that it has to answer to the people and not vice versa.' She turned to face Emily, who sat on the bed.

'I can understand your idealism, dear,' Emily said, 'but I'm afraid I agree with Congressman Winston. I'm not sure it will work. Oh, you might make a few points here and there. But you know how it is. Nothing remains the same. Once the commotion is over, things will go back to normal, and nobody will care. Even I know it takes a lot of publicity and media to force the public's attention onto things that need fixing. It's unfortunate, but I believe it's true.'

Susan laid her brush down carefully on the dresser. 'That's just it. We're fighting apathy. Oh, Em, maybe I am living in the wrong decade or even in the wrong century. We want people to wake up and care what happens to their country.'

'I know you do.'

'We want to prove that citizens really have a voice. That you can fight City Hall; that there is a right to information just like there is a right to speak out. We can't just let a few corrupt men run the world.'

'I can see that you feel very strongly about it. And I admire your dedication.'

Susan turned back to the mirror, searching for her bottle of liquid makeup and shaking it rather harder than she needed to get the makeup out.

'I'm afraid I'm not much help,' said Emily.

'Oh, I don't mean to be crying on your shoulder, Em. It's no one's problem but my own.'

Emily got up and rested a hand on Susan's shoulder. 'You were right to talk about it, Susan. I'd like to help you any way I can. Even if it means only listening.'

'Thanks, Em.'

'I'll leave you to get ready. And drink your

coffee before it gets cold.'

Susan finished applying her makeup and then put on the silk blouse and suit. As she stood before the mirror to inspect her appearance, she pursed her mouth together in an expression of dissatisfaction. She had succeeded in covering up the dark circles under her eyes, but it wasn't the look she wanted. The dark curls fell softly across her shoulders. Waves of hair flattered the contours of her face, and her lip liner made her lips look too inviting.

Hastily, she blotted the lipstick and sat down again. She pulled her hair back and swept it off her neck, twisting it into a chignon at the back of her head. Holding it there with one hand, she rummaged for pins in the dresser drawer and slid them into her hair to hold it in place, leaving only a few wispy curls at her ears. A touch more blusher and her cheekbones looked more prominent — determined. There, that was better.

She was still smoothing the hair into place when she heard the phone ringing downstairs. Who would call at eight-thirty in the morning? Geoffrey possibly, but she assumed he was busy getting ready for the hearing, as well.

She was just putting the last pin into place when Emily came running up the stairs.

'Susan, it's for you,' she called, opening the door without even a knock.

'Who — '

'Cindy, from your office. She sounded upset.'

Susan moved past Emily to the phone in the master bedroom. Picking it up, she said, 'Cindy, what is it?'

'Sue, it's Ted. He's been in an accident. The hospital just called. I came in early, and the phone was ringing — '

'Hospital.' Susan felt her heart in her throat. 'What condition — '

'He's unconscious. But you'd better go. Oh, Susan, what'll we do about the hearing?'

She swallowed, her throat was dry. 'Call Congressman Smith's office. You'll have to look up the number. Tell him I'm leaving for the hospital now. We won't be able to appear this morning. Maybe they can postpone it or something. Which hospital?'

'He's in George Washington University Hospital. Don't worry, Sue. I'll call Smith. Do you want me to come to the hospital?'

'No, stay there. I'll call you as soon as I know anything.' Susan hung up and ran back to her bedroom to find her shoes. Thank heavens Cindy had been there to take the call. Otherwise they might not have known for another hour.

'What is it?' Emily's face was as pale as Susan's.

'It's Ted. He's been in an accident. I've got to get to the hospital.'

'Can I do anything?'

'No, I'll be all right.'

'There'll be traffic on the roads now; be careful.'

'I will.' She rushed past Emily and down the stairs, grabbing her briefcase almost as an afterthought, though she didn't know what use she'd have for it now. Her only concern was for Ted. My God, unconscious! She tried to choke back the fear that raced through her. He might be dead. No, dear God, she prayed as she threw open her car door, got in and started the motor with trembling hands. She jerked the car away from the curb.

She drove as fast as she dared through the residential streets until she came to the red light at the main intersection. Her hands were ringing with perspiration now as she pictured Ted with sheets over him. An accident? Why? Ted was a good driver, in spite of his temper. And surely a minor fender bender, such as you might expect from rush-hour traffic, wouldn't have left him unconscious.

An ugly thought began to form. What if someone wanted to stop him from testifying this morning? Suppose something had gone wrong with his car just at the right time. An uneasy feeling crept up her spine, and she felt anger and rage so deep she was surprised at her own capacity for it. If the accident had been planned, she vowed to find out who had caused it, but the thoughts accompanying her desire for revenge unsettled even her. She felt like a mother lion facing a predator over a wounded cub. With her own bare hands she could kill the person who had been responsible for this, for deep in her heart she was sure that Ted himself was not at fault.

Traffic was heavy now as she came into the city. She wanted to lean on her horn, but she knew that would not help move the congested traffic any faster. Her heart pounded, and the hair that was so carefully pinned began to come loose. Her face was hot with the anger and frustration that coursed through her, and her hands were clammy as she gripped the wheel. How long had she been driving? Twenty minutes? And Ted was probably still in danger.

She had to make a conscious effort to slow her heart rate and keep her mind on the driving. She was so angry that she was in danger of smashing into the cars ahead of her as they slowed down to change lanes.

Finally, she was on Pennsylvania Avenue,

heading toward George Washington University Hospital. Five more minutes, she told herself.

An irrational thought forced its way into the back of her mind. Did Geoffrey know of this yet? It frightened her that his predictions about danger to them kept coming true. How did he know so much? Why did he have to be so right?

A chilling thought seized her. He couldn't possibly have anything to do with it himself, could he? It was impossible, but — And Ted had not believed Geoffrey innocent. Ted kept telling her Geoffrey would throw stumbling blocks in their path. Poor Ted. She hadn't believed him, and now he was lying in a coma in a hospital bed. But she knew that her thoughts, coming in snatches, weren't rational but motivated only by fear.

She was near the hospital complex now and slowed to turn into a parking garage. She jerked her window down and yanked at the parking ticket that a machine dispensed. Then she drove into the cavern, frantically looking for a parking place.

When at last she found a space and parked her car, she raced for the elevator that took her to the exit. It seemed like hours before she was in the sunlight again. Then she broke into a run, tripping once and slowing for fear she would twist an ankle in her dress shoes.

She sped past people milling around the entrance, went through the glass doors and, breathless, stopped at the reception desk. 'Ted Branagan. He was brought here an hour or so ago,' she said. 'Traffic accident. What room is he in?'

'One moment, please,' said the receptionist on duty. She consulted a clipboard. 'Branagan. I don't see . . . Did you say he was in an accident this morning?'

'Yes, yes,' Susan said, pleading silently for the woman to hurry.

'Let me check with emergency admitting.'

'Thank you.'

Susan clenched her fists waiting for the receptionist to speak into the phone. Then the woman looked up. 'Mr. Branagan is in intensive care. If you will wait here, Dr. Thompson will be right with you.'

She bit back her urgent request to see Ted, for she knew that hospitals were strict about their rules. She would just have to wait until this Dr. Thompson showed up.

She walked across to the bright green sofas where other friends and relatives of patients waited. How could she just sit here, she wondered, staring at a pregnant woman with her children across from her. Susan was looking hopefully at the entrance to the waiting area when Geoffrey walked in. She drew in her breath and rose as he came to her.

'I thought you'd be here,' he said. 'Ted?'

'I don't know. I haven't seen him yet.'

'Mr. Smith's office called. The session's cancelled.' He took her hands and pressed them in his. 'I'm sorry. Is there anything I can do?'

At Geoffrey's mention of the hearing, a thought struck her. She had been so concerned about Ted's well-being that up until now she had not inquired whether Ted's personal possessions had been accounted for. She knew he had been carrying the copies of the documents from which they'd planned to read that morning. He also had copies of Viktor Bruning's picture that they were going to exhibit. Ted had only picked them up yesterday after work, and Susan had not yet gotten her copies. The statement, of course, had been prepared ahead of time, but this bit of data about Globenet's Nazi presidents was new, and Bruning's photo in an SS uniform had just arrived from the Berlin Document Center. Susan had given it to Ted, and he'd had copies made.

If that photo could not be found, it would weaken their testimony. It would mean that they would have to request another copy of the original from the Berlin Document Center, and that would take time. But by then the hearing would be over, and Globenet would possibly retain its U.S. support for another year.

She stared stonily at Geoffrey. 'Someone's buying time.'

'I was afraid of that.' Then the compassion in his eyes turned to a hard glint as he looked down at her and said, 'Do you know what my first thought was when my secretary told me there had been an accident?'

She shook her head.

'I thought it could have been you.'

Yes, it could have been she. But it didn't make any difference. A deep anger seized her to think that someone would do this to any member of the AHG or anyone about to testify against a powerful organization jeopardizing freedoms of private citizens of the United States, and all for their own sordid reasons.

Their conversation was interrupted by the approach of a blond-haired man in a white coat.

'Miss Franks?' he said after casting an eye on the other people in the room and deciding Susan fit the description he had been given.

'Yes.' She whirled to face him.

'I'm Dr. Thompson. Mr. Branagan has just

regained consciousness. You may see him now, but only for a very few minutes. If you'll come with me.'

Geoffrey and Susan followed the doctor through the corridor where they caught an elevator to another floor. Susan barely noticed the dark blue-and-white-colored decor of the walls and the light blue carpets that kept the noise down. A nurse emerged from Ted's room and spoke briefly to the doctor; then, nodding to Geoffrey and Susan, she held the door for them to go in.

'I'll wait outside,' Geoffrey said, and Susan turned distractedly to him.

'All right.' Mercifully, he must have realized that if Ted saw him there, it would not help his physical or emotional well-being.

* * *

Susan walked slowly into the dimly lit room. Ted was lying very still in the bed nearest the window, a bandage wrapped around his head. His eyes were closed. Not wanting to wake him if he was sleeping, she walked quietly to the side of the bed. His breathing was even, and relief suddenly swept through her. She gripped the edge of the bed, suddenly feeling a little dizzy. Seeing a chair, she edged toward it. If she was going to faint, she wanted to do it while sitting down.

Ted's eyes fluttered open, and she moved back into his line of vision. 'Ted, it's me, Susan.'

He looked at her, and she could see him struggling to focus. She reached for his hand. 'Don't try to talk.'

He shook his head, and his voice sounded weak and husky. 'Glad you came,' he said. Then, turning his head toward her, he asked, 'What about the hearing?'

'The morning session is canceled. But don't think about that. You just think about getting better.'

He closed his eyes for a moment. Then Susan remembered about the briefcase. She hated to ask him any questions, but she had only five minutes, and it might be important. 'Ted?'

His eyes opened again. She leaned closer so he wouldn't have to strain to hear. 'Do you know what they did with the briefcase? You must have had the documents and photo with you in the car; the copies for the hearing.'

His eyelids raised. 'Don't know. Came here in an ambulance.' He squeezed her hand slightly. 'Got to get the documents and the photo to the committee. Will you?'

'Yes, Ted, yes. I'll take care of it, don't worry.' But even as she was soothing him back to sleep, an odd feeling was prickling at the back of her neck. She had to locate that photo quickly. She slid out of the room as quietly as she could.

Geoffrey questioned her with a look as soon as she emerged. But her thoughts were moving too fast for a complete explanation. 'He's all right, but I've got to find out what happened to the documents in his briefcase. There was a photo of Viktor Bruning in his SS uniform.'

She saw the glassed-in nurses' station at the end of the hall and headed in that direction. She stepped up to the desk.

'Excuse me,' she said to the nurse on duty there. 'There was a briefcase in the car with Mr. Branagan when he was injured. Would you know what became of it when the ambulance picked him up?'

The nurse shook her head. 'I'll call emergency and find out if any other personal possessions came in with him. They usually bring them with the patient to the room.'

The room. How stupid. She had forgotten to check Ted's room. She turned to Geoffrey.

'Geoffrey, I — '

'I'll wait here,' he said in his usual calm voice. 'You go and double-check Ted's room.'

She blinked once, saw the nurse calling on the telephone and fled back down the hall to

286

Ted's room. She stopped in front of the door, not wanting to wake him, then tiptoed in. A cursory glance told her his briefcase was not in view. She moved around the side of the bed to a metal closet and reached for the handle. It squeaked, making her shrink back against the window sill.

Ted moaned but didn't wake up. She saw that they'd hung his clothes there, and she flinched when she saw the blood on his shirt and suit jacket. She should take them away and get them cleaned. She could bring fresh clothes back when he was ready to go home.

She would do that, but not now. Now it was more important to find out what had become of the photo and documents they'd planned to use. Why would someone go to this trouble to get them? Even if they were stolen, Susan knew she could get hold of them again — she hoped. Unless the person who had them now had influence that reached as far as Berlin. She shivered at the thought. If what they had speculated about Globenet's Nazi connections were true, it might be possible. But it was a hideous thought.

No one would believe what they were prepared to tell the world without the documents and photograph to back them up.

Today was their chance to prove that Globenet had access to the intelligence files of the United States and was led by Nazis as late as 1972. Bruning's SS number and photograph of him in uniform would prove that. It was likely that the former Nazis who ran Globenet were pulling off something they didn't want the world to know about and so cluttered police files everywhere with false reports to keep the forces busy.

She looked in the nightstand, even under the bed, but the briefcase was nowhere to be found. Trying to squelch her disappointment, she stood up, and after looking closely at Ted to make sure he was all right, she eased out of the room again.

Geoffrey was coming down the hall. 'Any luck?' he asked.

'No. You?'

'Maybe. Come on.' He took her elbow and steered her toward the elevators. 'I spoke to emergency. The drivers who brought Ted in are out on another call. We can talk to them as soon as they come in. Right now we're going to the police.'

'We are?'

'To get access to the car.'

Of course. The police would have been there. Perhaps they had intercepted the briefcase.

'The car's been towed, but I've made arrangements for us to see it.'

She was gratified that it was so simple, but it grated on her that Geoffrey had obviously pulled bureaucratic strings to get them through. Yet she didn't voice her thoughts, afraid her irritability was getting the best of her. They needed to be efficient now, not to bicker.

She followed him out of the hospital to the parking garage, and they got into his car. In moments they were at the precinct, where they parked, then went inside. Geoffrey approached the desk, and a stocky sergeant looked up.

'I'm Congressman Winston. Lieutenant Hardesty is expecting us.'

The sergeant looked down at a chart and then hoisted himself out of his chair. His eyes flitted over Susan; then he said, 'This way.'

He led them down a hall and through another door to a room where several officers were at their desks, on telephones or typing reports. At a gray metal desk against a pillar in the middle of the room, a harried-looking, sandy-haired man was finishing with a phone call. The sergeant hitched up his belt as they waited.

When the lieutenant hung up, the sergeant

jerked his thumb over his shoulder. 'Congressman Winston here about that accident this morning.'

The lieutenant stuck out his hand, and Geoffrey shook it.

Then Susan said, 'We'd like to see the car Mr. Branagan was — ' she winced ' — pulled out of this morning. And we'd like to know if there was a briefcase found at the scene of the accident. Tan leather.'

The lieutenant frowned, then rifled through some papers on his desk. 'Here's the report. Dupont Circle. No, nothing about a briefcase. Anything valuable in it?'

Susan considered the possibilities. Whoever picked up the briefcase might not have known its contents. Still, if the police had gone through it, it was bound to raise a few eyebrows. If they chose to feed the information to Globenet ... But no, it was more likely that someone already knew what was in the briefcase and had staged the accident to intercept it.

'Just some papers he was going to give to me this morning. That's all,' she said.

The lieutenant continued going over the report, then said, 'I'll question the men who were first on the scene of the accident if you like.'

'Yes,' Susan said with a sinking heart. 'We'd

appreciate that.' But she knew that the briefcase was gone. They were given directions to where the car had been towed, thanked the lieutenant and left.

They rode silently to the garage. Once there, they quickly spotted Ted's Mustang. A mechanic was working on it from beneath. Susan realized they would have to have the car lowered to the ground to examine it. She started toward the mechanic, but Geoffrey's hand on her arm stopped her. His shoes scraped over the gritty floor as he approached the mechanic, who turned around and wiped his face with a dirty rag.

'We'd like to take a look in that car. Can you bring it down? I'm Congressman Winston. I believe the precinct called.'

'Just finished with this part, anyway.' The mechanic turned and bellowed to another man. 'Bring her down.'

As the car was being lowered, Susan asked, 'Would you know if there was anything in the car when it arrived here?'

Geoffrey already had the front door open when the mechanic shook his head. 'No, ma'am, not that I saw.'

'Thank you.'

It took them only a few minutes to realize there was nothing in the car. They even checked under the seats just in case anything had slid there. Susan stood up, the loss of all those weeks and months of work making her head throb. And when Geoffrey reached for her hand, it was ice cold.

'Come on, we might as well leave here,' he said.

With lead feet she followed him out to the car and got in. 'Where to now?' she asked dully.

'Back to the hospital. We have to talk to the ambulance drivers.'

'Oh, yes.' She had forgotten the ambulance drivers. Dared she hope they had seen something? She was grasping at straws for the smallest clue, and the tiny glimmer of hope within her was in danger of being smothered by the sense of defeat that already surrounded her.

12

Geoffrey let Susan out at the emergency entrance, then went to park the car. He had given her the names of the drivers to ask for, and now she approached a dark-haired nurse with olive skin and oval, slanted eyes.

'Excuse me,' Susan said. 'I need to see a Mr. Ray Blackburn, and a Mr. Donald Gregory, if they're back from their run. It's important.'

'Have a seat and I'll call them.'

Susan did not want to have a seat but decided it was best to play by their rules. She was sitting on the red plastic bench against the wall when Geoffrey came through the door. At the same time, the Oriental woman at the desk motioned to her, and Susan sprang up.

'Through that door,' she pointed. 'Mr. Blackburn and Mr. Gregory are outside.'

Evidently they'd finished their run. Geoffrey followed her through the door that led to a driveway. An ambulance sat parked near the sidewalk, but there was no activity around it. They walked to the front, and a young man of medium height in medic's garb was just closing the door to the driver's seat.

'Excuse me,' said Susan. 'I'm Susan Franks.' Then, seeing Geoffrey come up behind her, she said, 'and this is Congressman Winston. We wanted to ask you something about an accident this morning at Dupont Circle. You brought Ted Branagan here.'

'Yes,' said the young man. 'I remember. I'm Donald Gregory.'

She shook his hand. 'It's just that we were looking for something that Mr. Branagan had with him when he had the accident. We wondered if you'd seen it.' She felt her heart hammer as she watched the young man furrow his brow. *Please*, she prayed, *you're our last hope*.

'I'm not sure. What were you looking for?'

'A briefcase.' She felt like this was the hundredth time she had described it. 'It was tan leather, and he was bringing it to a meeting this morning.'

The young man thought, and she could see the apology in his eyes. Then he narrowed his eyes and stopped himself as he was about to speak. 'Wait a minute.' He shook his head. 'That's funny. I had forgotten it till now. You know how it is; you're so concerned for the patient.'

'What is it?'

'When the cops arrived, there was another man. I thought he was a plainclothesman, from the way he was acting. He looked in the car as soon as we got Mr. Branagan out. This man left with a briefcase. Tan leather, you say?'

Susan wanted to grab Donald Gregory by the shoulders, but she restrained herself, saying, 'Yes. Did you see it?'

'I don't know. I wasn't concentrating on anything but the patient. But this man might have carried off a briefcase. I remember because he didn't have anything in his hands at first. I know that because he helped the police keep the crowds back. He used his hands to do that. Both hands.' The young man shrugged. 'I don't know if that's much help.'

'It is a great deal of help,' said Geoffrey, who had moved closer. 'Now, can you tell us what this man looked like? The one who left with the briefcase.'

'Well, he was large, had sort of greasy-looking hair. I noticed his face — it was pockmarked, like he'd had severe acne or a disease that had left scars. Sorry, that's all I remember.'

Susan looked at Geoffrey, her eyes wide, her jaw slack. Pockmarked — the man in the library. 'Bradshaw,' she said. 'He has a man who fits that description.'

Geoffrey's eyes narrowed as he let out a hiss of air between his lips. Then his face took on its public mask, and he shook hands with the driver hastily, saying, 'Thank you very much. You've been a big help.' Then he said to Susan, 'Come on.' He grabbed her arm, and she nearly cried out from the fierceness of his grasp.

If he was thinking what she was thinking, they had no time to lose. 'Is it?' she asked as she nearly had to run to keep up.

'Bradshaw, yes. He's got to be orchestrating all this,' Geoffrey said in an angry voice. They dashed around the building and headed for the parking lot. Geoffrey ran ahead to the Audi, and by the time Susan got to the car, he had the motor running. She waited until he had backed out, then climbed in. He twisted the steering wheel, then lunged forward, tires screeching as the car took the corner. She tightened her grip on the seat, and when they had to slow down to pay the parking toll, she fastened her seat belt, for she knew they would have to race against time now.

Geoffrey unhooked the telephone from its receiver on the dashboard and handed it to Susan. 'We've got to get the police. The number's on a card in the glove compartment.'

She looked. 'Here it is,' she said.

'Tell them to send a car to this address.' He gave her a street address in Falls Church, which she repeated to herself. Susan did as she was told and explained over the phone that this was an emergency.

'I'm with Congressman Geoffrey Winston,' she said. 'It's regarding the accident this morning at Dupont Circle. A leather briefcase was stolen from the site of the accident.'

The dispatcher said they would have someone there within ten minutes. Susan replaced the phone and hung on for dear life as Geoffrey darted through traffic and turned onto the highway. He was speeding now, for his main objective was to get to Bradshaw before it was too late. With the hearing called off, it was the perfect opportunity for Bradshaw to make his escape. With the photo and documents the pock-marked man must have brought him, Bradshaw was buying time for the Globenet elite, the men who pulled the strings. And if they didn't catch him, he would disappear. Geoffrey considered the airport, but without the help of the police they had no way of knowing what flight he might take.

'Bradshaw is our link,' Geoffrey said as they took a flat stretch of highway.

'Of course. I should have seen that myself.'

'He wasn't that obvious. He's had others working for him.'

Susan thought about the shadow at the end of the hall the night the elevator broke down, the face at the window, even the incidents she'd dismissed before, such as the car that had bumped her, then driven off that day.

Geoffrey was going on. 'This morning I got confirmation of large sums of money being transferred into Bradshaw's bank account.' He threw a swift look at Susan. 'I'm sorry about Ted. Now I know he's not in on it.'

'How?'

'I found the records. He was falsely arrested twelve years ago for a bomb scare at Stapleton International Airport. He was innocent, but the police made such a mess of the affair that when someone in Globenet offered to handle the whole thing for him in exchange for working for them, he took them up on it.'

'He never told me.'

'He was young and impressionable. They probably persuaded him that he could best help his country by informing on others who might be engaged in illegal activities, no matter how small. The Globenet officials paid him and claimed to use the information for bona fide police investigations. They used knowledge gained from hundreds of such informants to throw suspicion on small-time criminals, keeping attention away from their own illegal activities. But he finally got fed up and left the country. My private investigator unearthed his letter of resignation. It made it clear to me that he was through with them.'

'Then that's why he went to Europe?'

'To escape their clutches. Then through the AHG, he must have been fighting back. I was mistaken about that. I thought Globenet might have planted him there to make sure the AHG didn't get too close. And I still suspected he might have set everything up that happened. This morning proved I was wrong.'

Stunned relief combined with racing adrenaline as it began to sink in that Geoffrey was admitting he had been wrong about Ted. Still, she couldn't help a tiny sliver of resentment that surfaced. If only he had discovered this bit of evidence sooner, they might have been able to avoid this morning's accident.

'What put you onto Bradshaw?' she asked as Geoffrey took the exit to Falls Church.

'I tried to trace his personal business

dealings. I had the feeling he had more money than a congressman ought to have. It appeared someone was lining his pocket. Probably someone whose interest he was supposed to protect in Congress.'

'Globenet.'

'Yes. And I had to play devil's advocate with you so Bradshaw and his cronies wouldn't be frightened off before they were caught. Can you forgive me?'

'Of course. I only wish I could have helped you. I wish I had known.'

'I was afraid for you, and I didn't think you'd want to go prying into your friend's background,' he admitted. 'I knew if there was evidence against Ted, I'd have to find it myself. But I'm sorry. I misjudged him.'

She drew her brows together in a puzzled frown. 'But what did Bradshaw get out of it?'

'Most likely they had something on him, blackmailing him into cooperating. Or else they'd promised him power, a say in the operation. I think we can lay our fingers on it now. There are honest law-enforcement officials who will be anxious to question him.'

She braced herself against the dashboard as Geoffrey ran a stop sign at the end of the exit ramp and swung into a circular street that led past stately Georgian homes set far back on manicured lawns.

Geoffrey continued. 'If Globenet succeeded in wrapping up the information on
the entire world, it would be just one more
step to world domination, wouldn't it? And
Bradshaw would collect his rewards.'

'And with their Nazi background . . . ' She
shivered at the implication.

'I was worried about you, Susan; you'll
never know how much. But I hoped Globenet
wouldn't want to draw attention to themselves by taking drastic measures. I knew they
wouldn't really — ' He couldn't finish.

Her face was drained of color. 'There's a
word for that, isn't there? I think they
eliminate those who stand in their way.'

His face was grim, the lines deep around
his mouth. 'But that sort of thing would bring
too much publicity. At least I prayed that was
their thinking. Especially since you were
so . . . ' He searched for the right words.

'I know. Adamant.' She touched his knee
and spoke in a hushed tone. 'I'm sorry. You
were right.'

They turned into the drive of a three-story
brick house just as a long black limousine was
backing out. Geoffrey swung the Audi across
the driveway, preventing the limo from
moving farther. The driver of the limo got
out, and Susan was stunned to recognize the
blond man who'd moved in across the street

from her. But before he could utter a word, Geoffrey went around to the passenger side and opened the door. There he met the glare of Irwin Bradshaw.

'What do you think you're doing, Winston? I could have you arrested for trespassing on private property.'

'I've already called the police, Bradshaw,' he said. 'And I'm going to give them this.' He reached in and extracted Ted's briefcase.

Susan uttered a small gasp and took the briefcase as he handed it to her, then watched in amazement as Geoffrey reached into the limousine and pulled Irwin Bradshaw out.

'I wouldn't try anything if I were you,' said Geoffrey, and at that instant the blare of sirens announced two police cars. They turned into the driveway and pulled to a stop, red lights flashing.

'What the — ' Bradshaw sputtered as the cops got out.

'Officers, arrest this man for possession of stolen goods. This briefcase was stolen this morning out of an '84 Mustang at Dupont Circle. The documents in it belong to the Association for Honesty in Government. We have witnesses.'

'Take him, too,' Susan said, pointing to the chauffeur, the scar under his eye turning beet red. 'For questioning.'

Bradshaw was about to protest, but even before the policemen could tell him his rights, he seemed to think better of speaking. Susan could see it in the narrowing of his eyes and the grim set to his mouth. He silenced the blond chauffeur with a look. His only comment was to Geoffrey.

'You think you're so righteous, Winston. You may regret this.'

The way he said it sent a chill down Susan's spine, but the look of certainty on Geoffrey's face made her straighten her stance. The rat was caught in the trap.

As the police led Bradshaw and the chauffeur away, Geoffrey motioned for Susan to get back in the car. 'That's all we can do here.'

Susan took a deep breath and slumped against the back of the seat. 'We were lucky.'

'Yes, very,' said Geoffrey. 'I wasn't sure which way he'd jump. But I knew we'd never catch up with him at the airport, if that's where he was headed. Something told me he was so sure of himself he would take his time.' He glanced at her. 'He didn't count on our finding out who took the briefcase. Only you could have made that connection.'

She was still stunned at the events of this morning, shaking with the aftermath of shock. But gradually everything was falling into place. The threats — Bradshaw's little army.

'Thank goodness we've got these,' she said, holding the documents and photo in her hands. All the copies were there, too.

Geoffrey threw her a questioning glance. 'Do you think you can — '

'Testify in Ted's place?' She lifted her chin. 'Yes, of course.'

'Good. We'll let Mr. Smith know you're prepared to testify at the afternoon session.' A sardonic smile curved his lips. 'You were afraid I would attack you in public again, weren't you?'

'Well, yes, but I hoped not.'

He reached over and gave her hand a quick squeeze. 'I was always on your side,' he said more softly. 'You just didn't know it.'

'Yes, I know that now.'

They drove back to the city at a more leisurely pace. They had time to eat in the cafeteria in the Rayburn Building before the session, and Susan forced herself to swallow, even though her stomach was collecting butterflies. Now everything was in her hands. How well would she be able to present the evidence? Would she be convincing?

Geoffrey seemed to be thinking as they ate. When he finished his cup of coffee, he looked hard at her. 'And Ted?'

She couldn't quite interpret the meaning of the question, but she could see the doubt in his eyes. 'What about him?' she asked.

Geoffrey's eyes shielded his expression warily as he said, 'Your loyalty to him — it is still deep, isn't it?'

Then she understood. Geoffrey still did not know that her feelings for Ted ended with friendship and common cause. She had nothing of the intimacy and sharing with Ted that was growing daily between Geoffrey and her.

'Oh, Geoffrey,' she said, reaching toward him. 'There's no comparison. He will always be my friend, but I've never loved him, not the way I . . . ' His eyes locked with hers, and his soul seemed to open to her.

★ ★ ★

At two p.m. the congressional Subcommittee on U.S. Involvement with Globenet convened. Susan felt very much in the spotlight as she sat at the polished table waiting to speak. Congressman Ernest Smith summarized the facts they already knew. Globenet was a private organization with 135 member countries. It had no power of arrests but was a clearinghouse for information on criminal suspects. Now they would hear additional evidence presented by Susan Franks for the Association for Honesty in Government. Other witnesses would follow, including the head of the U.S. branch of Globenet. By the close of the hearings, the committee would recommend whether or not the United States should continue to support the agency. He reminded members of the subcommittee that half a million dollars a year of the taxpayers' money was at stake.

Susan took her place behind the microphone. She drew a breath and began her statement, presenting the facts in order. Globenet, though a private organization with voluntary international membership, had access to government intelligence files through the Treasury Enforcement Communications System. These data were shared with their member countries, which included dictatorships, totalitarian governments and countries behind the Iron Curtain. Through its communication system, Globenet passed information to twenty thousand local and state police units. She reminded the subcommittee that Globenet was founded in 1935 in Vienna and continued through the Second World War. She held up copies of their *Police Journal* dated 1939, 1941 and 1944. So quite clearly, Globenet was in Nazi hands during the war.

After the war, Globenet's files were turned over to Allied authorities, but the files were never purged. Globenet's secretary-general had refused to use Globenet's network to hunt Nazi war criminals, and Susan quoted, 'The Nazi crimes were political, and Globenet's constitution prevents them from intervention in any political, military, religious or racial matters.'

Halfway through her statement, she risked a glance at Geoffrey. Her lips formed a half smile, and his eyes radiated warmth and support. The other members of the subcommittee, so often in these hearings failing to pay attention, all looked alert with rapt attention. It caused her to sit even straighter and project her voice with more certainty.

Finally, she reached her conclusion. Globenet had had Nazi presidents. She held up the photo of Viktor Bruning wearing an SS uniform. 'Viktor Bruning was president of Globenet from 1966 through 1972,' she said. 'With half a million taxpayers' dollars a year, the percentage of requests through Globenet's channels that lead to arrest is only eighteen. Is this merely a high degree of inefficiency, or is Globenet guilty of greater crimes?

'Gentlemen, I suggest to you that Globenet keeps the eyes of the world on small-time criminals in order to protect its own major ones. They prey on two kinds of individuals: those they believe to be enemies of Globenet's neo-Nazi bent, and those who merely have the bad luck to be in the way; men and women who unknowingly offer possibilities for Globenet to use them. Either way, this seems to point up the contempt these Globenet officials have for human rights. Until further investigation can prove or disprove this, I strongly urge you to withdraw U.S. support from this organization, which has such questionable credentials.'

She sat down to applause, another rarity at subcommittee hearings. A flush swept over her. Ted's accident was partially avenged. It would be fully avenged when she saw Irwin Bradshaw indicted for theft, embezzlement or whatever else he was guilty of and forced to reveal his illicit connections to Globenet's higher echelons.

No one had any questions, and approving glances came her way as she listened to a second witness, who also spoke of Globenet's unscrupulous actions. But it was Geoffrey's smile she sought when he caught up with her in the hall outside. His eyes bathed her with pride as he took her arm and bent to kiss her lightly on the cheek.

'Geoffrey,' she said in astonishment. 'Here?'

'Why not?' he said in an undertone. 'They'll be reading the announcement in the newspapers soon enough.'

'What announcement?'

'Our engagement, of course. That is — ' he looked contrite for a moment ' — if you're willing.'

'Geoffrey Winston, what nerve.' But she couldn't help the laughter that threatened as they made their way to the elevator, and he walked her out into the sunlight. The sun was dropping toward the horizon, and the scent of honeysuckle drifted toward them. Spring was going to give way to warmer months, to soft summer evenings.

'Well?' he asked as they stood on the sidewalk.

'Well what?'

'Well, you haven't answered me.'

'You haven't asked me.'

He twisted his mouth in wry amusement. 'All right, we'll have it your way. Miss Franks, may I have the honor of your hand in marriage?'

She couldn't resist his teasing, but this time she knew that the butterflies in her stomach were not caused by a public performance she would have to give. 'Yes, you may,' she said.

Then he encircled her with his arms — those arms that gave her so much support.

'Do you think you'll like being a congress-man's wife? Politics can be deadly, you know.'

She answered him easily, her heart full and her mind sure. 'I'll like whatever we choose to tackle,' she said, 'together.' Then in a sexy voice, she added, 'I'll take you, Mr. Winston, congressman or not.'

'And how will you like taking on a family of two strapping adolescents?'

She smiled, already eager to meet the boys this man had fathered. 'They can't be any harder to take on than the U.S. government.'

Geoffrey raised his eyebrows. 'I wouldn't be so sure. They can be mighty challenging at times.' His look softened, and he lowered his mouth again to taste her cheek and lips. 'They can only love you a fraction as much as I do. But even that will be a lot.'

Susan returned his kiss, then realized they were probably stopping traffic by now. She pulled away and tugged on his arm, heading down the sidewalk. 'Come on,' she said. 'We've got things to do.'

We do hope that you have enjoyed reading this large print book.

Did you know that all of our titles are available for purchase?

We publish a wide range of high quality large print books including:
Romances, Mysteries, Classics
General Fiction
Non Fiction and Westerns

Special interest titles available in large print are:
The Little Oxford Dictionary
Music Book
Song Book
Hymn Book
Service Book

Also available from us courtesy of Oxford University Press:
Young Readers' Dictionary
(large print edition)
Young Readers' Thesaurus
(large print edition)

For further information or a free brochure, please contact us at:
Ulverscroft Large Print Books Ltd.,
The Green, Bradgate Road, Anstey,
Leicester, LE7 7FU, England.
Tel: (00 44) **0116 236 4325**
Fax: (00 44) **0116 234 0205**

Other titles published by
The House of Ulverscroft:

PRAIRIE FIRE

Patricia Werner

In 1887, in the ranchlands of the Oklahoma territory, the beautiful Kathleen Calhoun is ready to start a life of her own. A chance meeting brings the handsome Raven Sky into her life. Sky is gentle and educated, but he is also a Creek Indian . . . Kathleen's attraction to Raven Sky is undeniable, but her dreams are haunted by the Indian savages who brutally murdered her parents. Torn, Kathleen flees Oklahoma and the arms of her beloved. Deep within, she knows she must return to the firm embrace of Raven Sky to feed the flames of her desire . . .